Books by the author:

The Poetry of Henry Newbolt:
   Patriotism Is Not Enough   critical biography

What I Cannot Say to You   stories

Small

Displacements

Vanessa
Furse Jackson

Livingston Press
The University of West Alabama

isbn 13: 978-1-60489-050-1 library binding
isbn 13: 978-1-60489-051-8 trade paper
Library of Congress Control Number 2010920378
Printed on acid-free paper.
Printed in the United States of America,
United Graphics
Hardcover binding by: Heckman Bindery
Typesetting and page layout: Joe Taylor
Cover design and layout: Joe Taylor
Cover art: Mark Anderson, who may be reached at
mark.anderson@tamucc.edu
Proofreading: Connie James, Joe Taylor, Tricia Taylor

This is a work of fiction.
Any resemblance
to persons living or dead is coincidental.

Livingston Press is part of The University of West Alabama,
and thereby has non-profit status.
Donations are tax-deductible:
brothers and sisters, we need 'em.

first edition
6 5 4 3 2 1

Table of Contents

The Wild Dogs   1

Miss Best and Mr. Marvel   24

Rain   35

The Clinic   50

A Nice Day Out   62

Before the Fall   74

The Albert Memorial   86

Grieving for Man   96

Consequences   112

The Stand-in   129

Small Displacements   142

For my mother,
Jane Furse

Small

Displacements

The Wild Dogs

"We should get some of those sacks of lime that are lying behind the cow barn and dump it on a few flower beds," Dylan said. "Do some real damage, that would."

"They're too heavy to lift," said Belinda. She was always sparring with Dylan, as if he, not Terry, were her brother.

"Not if we borrow my mum's cheese cart," Dylan said. This was a large box with a long handle, mounted on two old wheelbarrow wheels, that his mum used to transport her goat cheeses to the village shop my parents ran.

We were huddled around a fire in a bit of waste ground beyond Arcadia Avenue, staring gloomily at the houses that looked stark and obscene, built as they had been on our turf, our country, our Comanche stalking grounds. Old Bracey had sold his farm-land to the developers for some fantastic sum, we'd heard. Stupid old man.

1976 was one of the hottest summers on record, and we hardly needed the fire for warmth, but we were drawn to fires as filings to a magnet, and no meeting was ever held without one. The waste ground, strewn with discarded lengths of wood, broken bricks, and piles of sand from the building works, had become our headquarters that year. All the better to keep an eye on the enemy from.

"What about getting some muck from the old slurry pit?" Benny said. "That's really squiffy stuff."

"Yeah," his brother said. Hedgehog, like me, was a follower. Benny and Hedgehog were twins. Their dad kept the Shell garage at which the men from the Avenue filled up their Rovers and Humbers for the morning commute to London.

"Wouldn't do your mum's cheeses much good," Terry said to Dylan.

"Can't make them smell worse than they do already," Belinda said. "Goat's cheese, peee-ugh!"

"Shut up, you lot," Dylan said. "I'm thinking." His freckles were standing out against his pale face, as they always did when he was absorbed in something. He had red hair and thin-looking skin, and he never went brown in the summer like the rest of the gang. Dylan was my friend, my idol, tough and inventive, the free spirit that I aspired to be as I trailed in his dangerous, heroic wake.

Fat Terry dug in his shorts pocket and passed round a tube of Spangles. He was generous like that. We sucked and crunched as Dylan continued to think.

"'Don't go breaking my heart,'" Belinda sang. That was the great Elton John/Kiki Dee hit of that summer. Belinda had a nice voice. "'I couldn't if I tried','" she sang back to herself, jiggling her head so her short mousy curls riffled and bounced.

"You heard the man. Shut *up*," said Benny.

"Yeah," said Hedgehog, giving her a push.

Belinda stopped singing and walloped Hedgehog in the stomach. "Don't touch me, you little prick," she said.

Terry giggled.

"Hey," Benny said.

Hedgehog was bent over, hands on his stomach, his half-sucked Spangle covered with dusty earth on the ground beside him. I could see the tears in his eyes.

"Leave Belinda alone," Dylan said, aware, as I was, that Benny was itching for vengeance. I was aware, too, of the unspoken link between Dylan and Belinda that this summer had acquired a new strand of tension to it. I tried to puzzle it out because it was the kind of link I wanted with him—an indivisible, two-as-one link—but had never quite achieved.

"'When I was down / I was your clown','" Belinda sang, poking the fire with a charred stick so that sparks swirled up from it.

"You want to be careful," Benny said. "Ground's as dry as tinder at the moment."

"Go teach your grandma to suck eggs," Belinda retorted, poking again.

"It's going to have to be well after dark," Dylan said, his narrow blue eyes very bright. "Can you all get away tonight? JJ?"

He looked at me because he knew it was hardest for me. I lived with my mum and dad in cramped rooms over the shop, which made it tricky to sneak out at night. But there was no way I was going to be left out of a Wild Dog expedition, specially not as I knew Belinda would be right there behind Dylan. "Course," I said. "What time?"

"Is this a private fire, or can anybody join?" said a man's voice from behind us, and we all froze. Where adults were concerned, we tended to feel guilty first and ask why later.

Dylan turned cautiously. "What do you want?" he asked.

The man came around the fire and folded himself up on the rough dry grass. "Entertainment," he said.

"Pardon?" Belinda said.

"I'm bored," the man said, looking at her. "So I came in search of entertainment."

We looked at each other. "Came from where?" Dylan asked.

"I live up the road," the man said. "House called Sea Drift."

Benny made a surreptitious sick noise. All the houses in Arcadia Avenue had putrid names like that. Our village was over seventy miles from the sea, about as far inland as you can get in England.

"It belongs to my parents, in actual fact," the man said. "They've just retired. Sea Drift being their idea of a dream home, you understand." His eyes, I noticed, were a very pale blue.

"Oh, yes?" Dylan said.

"My father had a boat called Sea Drift once," the man said, as if apologizing for his parents' taste. "A yacht, actually."

"Oh, a yacht," Dylan said, and I could tell by the way he pronounced the word that he was mocking the speaker.

Perhaps the man could, too, because he took out a packet of cigarettes—Benson and Hedges King Size—and offered them around. With our limited funds, we only ever bought Players No. 6 from the machine down the side of the Shell garage when Benny and Hedgehog's dad was busy with a customer. We each took one, except Terry who didn't smoke, and the man lit them for us with a Zippo whose pale tongue of flame stank of lighter fluid in the hot sun.

"I'm Alan," the man said. "Alan Manson." His jeans had a crease ironed into the front of each leg, and his T-shirt had a collar.

"I'm Belinda," Belinda said, sitting cross-legged and very straight. "And these boys here . . ."

You could tell by her tone that she was implying *children*, as if she was no longer one of us. I stared over the man Alan's head as she introduced each of us to him.

"JJ," he said. "Standing for what?"

No one ever asked me that. It was my name. JJ.

"Jay Jalal," Belinda said, tossing her short curls. "Jay Jalal Baker."

"How unlikely," Alan said, blowing a smoke ring that Hedgehog watched with his mouth open.

My mother's Kurdish family had left Turkey after World War Two, tired of being always watchful, always labelled as second-class citizens. It wasn't, she'd told me in her pretty, sing-song voice, so very much better here. But she loved my big English dad, and the local people had got used to her behind the counter in the shop. None of the villagers would have said *how unlikely* in quite those tones. I didn't like the man Alan, I decided.

"We're the Wild Dogs," Belinda said.

"Are you, indeed?" Alan Manson said, with just a hint of amusement in his voice.

Dylan looked at Belinda as if he'd have liked to muzzle her, his freckles dark on his face. "Thanks for the cigarettes," he said politely, putting out the end of his with a stone and stashing the stogie in his shorts pocket. "We need to be going, though. We have business to attend to." He stood up.

"Thanks very much," Benny said, standing rather reluctantly, I thought.

"Yeah," said Hedgehog.

"Anytime," Alan said, remaining seated by the dying fire.

"Bye then, Mr. Manson," Belinda said.

I managed to creep out undetected for our midnight rendezvous that night, my heart thumping as if it was only just managing to stay behind my skin. The drainpipe seemed looser on the wall than usual, the store-room roof below more fragile, but no window was flung up, no lights switched on, and I got to the waste ground before anyone but Dylan. He was always there first, waiting for us to gather. "Let's hope no more of *them* come looking for entertainment tonight," he whispered to me.

"I didn't like him," I said.

Vanessa Furse Jackson

"Wanting in the gang," Dylan said with scorn. "As if he could at his age."

He was probably in his twenties, but to us Alan Manson had seemed old—squarely on the other side of the un-crossable divide that fences off generations from one another.

Dylan had brought two cans of black paint and a block of putty in an old frayed duffle bag, which he squatted on the dark ground to open and show me. I never asked him where he got his supplies. Anything we needed he seemed to spirit from the air—it was one of the gifts that kept me bound to his side. I sometimes wished I had the nerve to pinch something we needed from my parents' shop, but my dad would have thrashed the daylights out of me if he'd caught me. Climbing out of my bedroom window at night was as far as I dared to go. And my heart was still beating at twice its normal rate.

"Benny's bringing brushes," Dylan said, in a half-whisper. "We'll have to do the putty with our hands."

"Which end do we start?" I asked, trying to harden my jaw against the shameful chattering of my teeth.

"The far end, I reckon. Work our way back to here." Dylan put a hand out and touched my arm. "It's going to be our best yet, JJ," he said. "It can't fail."

I felt a flush of closeness to him, and my jaw loosened. "Best ever," I agreed.

"Wild Dogs gotta stick together," Dylan muttered.

African wild dogs, or painted dogs, are never alone. They're intensely social, living their whole lives in close contact with their pack mates. Now an endangered species, they're vulnerable to canine diseases but most of all to man—to white hunters, on whose exotic game preserves they poach, and to wealthy industrialists, whose diamond mining diverts the water the dogs need to survive.

When the others arrived, Benny and Hedgehog with the promised brushes, we set off on a long loop that took us through the scrubby ground behind the raw new gardens on one side of Arcadia Avenue. It was very dark, and my plimsolls kept stubbing unseen tussocks of grass on the lumpy ground. Once, Terry put his foot in a rabbit hole and measured his padded length on the ground with a sudden *oof*. At the top of the Avenue, we split up, Dylan taking Belinda and Terry to do one side, and me going with Benny and Hedgehog down the other. I wanted to believe that Dylan was entrusting me as his second-in-command, and I resented Benny's commandeering of the paint pot, but I didn't say so.

Our job was to exterminate every house sign all the way down the Avenue. Four Winds, The Captain's Cabin, Dunkirk, Dunworkin, The Laurels, The Larches, The Presbytery, Mon Repos, Sea Drift, The Great Escape, and many more whose names I've long forgotten—all painted and puttied to oblivion. There were slate signs, wood-carved signs, stone signs, iron, painted, tiled, pottery, and brass signs. The only one that defeated us that night was the wrought-iron scrollwork of Bishop's Court. All the rest we blackened out, puttying them flat first if the name appeared in relief then painting them over with furious licks of Benny's brushes. We scurried from one to the next, sometimes running back to give a difficult sign a second coat, keeping our eyes on the other half of the gang over the road, staying parallel to them as best we could. Only once did Benny, Hedgehog and I freeze, smelling an unexpected whiff of cigarette smoke, but although we stood still as gateposts in the shadows, we couldn't hear anything move, so we crept on to the next house, sweating but undiscovered.

It was one of the best stunts we'd ever pulled, and when we got back to the waste ground, we were high as goal scorers, slapping each other on the back and laughing, Terry attempting to muffle his insane giggle with both hands. I saw Belinda throw her arms around Dylan, but he wriggled free and shook my hand, and none of us wanted to call it a night and slink home to bed again. We thrust the almost empty paint pots and the brushes deep into a pile of broken two-by-fours and cleaned our hands as best we could on the rough grass. We hadn't thought to bring white spirit, of course, and all of us, it turned out, had black spots on our jeans and shoes that later had to be picked off and explained away. But not one of us was caught. It was a triumph.

The next morning I stacked shelves in the shop while my dad did accounts at his desk in the store room and my mother talked to customers in the sweetly-accented English that embarrassed me only when she came to my school, timid and effacing, and singled me out as the *other* I tried so hard not to be. In the shop, she was on her own ground, knowledgeable and in charge, even if she did keep her eyes lowered much of the time. She was that nice little Mrs. Baker who stocked everything you could possibly want

Vanessa Furse Jackson

in a valiant rearguard action against the delicatessen, the health food shop, the supermarkets spreading like sores through the local towns. I stacked my shelves, and I listened.

"Bloody kids."

"Did you hear?"

"Have you seen what they did?"

"Vandalism, pure and simple."

"Two hours to get it off."

"Don't talk to me about the police."

"She weren't 'alf angry."

"S'all that TV, if you ask me."

"Really, it's too bad."

"Nothing like this in my day."

Gleefully, I fiddled with stacks of Quaker Oats and Bird's Custard and stored up the buzz of gossip to take with me later to The Wild Dogs.

"You keep an eye on that boy of yours, Mrs. Baker."

"Oh my Jay—he's a good boy, a good boy."

"It's the company they fall in with, Mrs. Baker, you mark my words."

When, last to arrive, I fell in with the gang that afternoon, there was no fire, and Dylan was anxious to leave the waste ground. "It's too close to *them*," he said. "We don't want to be seen here today. Besides . . ."

"That man," I said.

"Mr. Weirdo. Come on. We'll go to the gypsy dump instead. It's cooler there, anyway."

The gypsy dump, another favoured haunt of ours, was in the steep strip of woodland below where Dylan lived with his hippy-dippy mum and dad in a run-down bungalow that had once belonged to old Bracey's cowman. I don't know whether gypsies had ever camped in the vicinity, but there was certainly a rubbish dump half dug into the side of a bank, from which old pram wheels, food tins, bottles, dead shoes, bits of rotting cloth and soggy carpet protruded like ill-buried casualties of some forgotten battle.

We made a ring of stones and started a fire from dry leaves and twigs and shards from a wooden banana box, then squatted around it, watching the thin ripples of flame. Terry passed round a tube of Refreshers, and we sucked at their tart fizz, trapping them against the roofs of our mouths till they melted into tiny crunchy pieces between our teeth.

"Our mum says she's sure it was the kids from the council estate who did it," Belinda said.

"It was all they were talking about in the shop this morning," I said, and told them what I could remember.

Dylan hugged his knees. "Perfect," he kept saying. "Just perfect."

"You should have heard our dad," Benny said. "On and on about it. 'If I thought any child of mine . . .'" He and Hedgehog rolled onto their backs laughing.

"We should have left a sign, Dyl," Belinda said, chewing on a twig with her sharp white teeth. She hadn't yet lost the habit of doing things she thought made her seem more like a boy. From where I sat, though, I could see the little breasts beneath her yellow Aertex shirt that said she was plumb out of luck. However short she cut her hair, however much she swaggered and swore, Belinda was all girl. She scared me a bit, to tell you the truth.

"You daft or what?" said Dylan, who didn't like other people to come up with ideas he hadn't thought of first. "You *want* people to know it was us?"

"I said a sign, not a signature, stupid."

Benny sat up and thumped her shoulder. "Watch it, Belly."

She hated it when he called her that. Her hand went up to hit him, but Hedgehog grabbed her wrist before she could, and he and Benny had her pinned to the ground in seconds, wriggling and kicking and spitting up into their faces. I thought it wouldn't be long before they got their revenge for her walloping Hedgehog yesterday.

Terry giggled and popped three Refreshers into his mouth at once. Dylan looked at me and rolled his eyes.

"Pax," she finally yelled. "Pax, you pair of cretins. Let me *go*."

The three of them sat up, Belinda scarlet in the face and rubbing her wrists. Benny and Hedgehog were panting, their eyes bright and excited.

"Now, now, children," said Dylan.

"I've a good mind to go home and leave you bunch of pissing apes to it," Belinda said.

"What kind of a sign?" Dylan asked her.

"Never mind," she said.

"Like write *The Wild Dogs woz 'ere*, or something, d' you mean?"

"A paw print," Belinda said, sulkily. "I thought just a paw print would do."

Vanessa Furse Jackson

"Good idea, Bel," Dylan said, which I thought was big of him. "The sign of the paw print. I like it. We should leave it everywhere we go."

"Well, hi, here you are," said Alan Manson, and sat down by the fire.

I heard Dylan's breath go out in a whoosh of surprise.

"Well, hi, Mr. Manson," said Belinda, all honey. "What brings you here?"

"Alan, please. I saw the smoke from your fire," the man said. "Elementary, my dear Watson."

"Huh?" Terry said.

Dylan looked furious, as if Alan was deliberately exposing the incompetence of his leadership.

"So what are the Wild Dogs up to after last night's little escapade?" Alan said. He got out his packet of B & H and ceremoniously handed them round. Belinda, Benny and Hedgehog each accepted one. I wasn't going to if Dylan wasn't.

"I don't what you're talking about," Dylan muttered, his eyes on the fire.

"Oh, come on," Alan said.

"It was you," Benny said, his voice big with discovery.

I remembered the smell of cigarette smoke in the dark and our sweaty fear.

"What was?" Hedgehog asked.

"I watched you for most of the way," Alan said. "Good entertainment. I told you I got bored easily."

"Cool Comanche!" Benny said, with a reverence I thought was wholly misplaced.

"Wow," echoed Hedgehog.

"Trust you three to get seen," Belinda said scornfully.

"So, are you going back tonight to leave your paw print?" Alan asked.

I felt rather as I had when we first realized that they really were going to rip up half a mile of our secret countryside to put giant mansions on— puny, helpless, and mad at being made to feel that way. If Alan knew all that, the gang was eviscerated, done for. There didn't seem much point in it any more.

"None of your business what we do," said Terry, taking half a packet of melting Rolos from his shorts pocket and beginning to peel off the stuck foil.

"Mind your lip, Smelly Tel," Belinda said, punching his arm hard.

Terry picked up the Rolos he'd dropped, succeeded in freeing them from the foil, and put them all into his mouth without offering one to any of us.

I watched him chew the huge sweet mouthful, admiring his independence.

"We aren't stupid kids, you know," Dylan said.

"No, of course not," Alan said. "Last night's sortie proved that. A brilliant execution, if I may say so."

Terry chewed. Dylan stared at the fire, his freckles black against his skin.

"He saw you, and you didn't know he was there?" Belinda said, still with that edge of scorn in her voice.

"We smelled his cigarette smoke," I said.

Alan looked at me out of his pale blue eyes, as if I'd just sneaked on him to the fuzz or something. "It got me thinking," he said.

"Thinking what?" Belinda asked him, sitting cross-legged and straight-backed, as if she was aware the little breasts stuck out better like that.

"A good sortie, as I said. Well executed. But . . ." He took a long drag of his cigarette.

Hedgehog grinned at the ensuing smoke ring.

I wasn't going to ask what the word sortie meant. It sounded demeaning, like a nickname for something we'd done in deadly earnest.

"But?" Belinda said, leaning her straight back forward from the hips in that way only girls can.

"I think the Wild Dogs could do better than that," he said. "With some help, naturally."

"Naturally," said Dylan.

Which was how we came to do the most criminal thing we'd done since the gang came together. Why we all agreed, I'm still not sure, except that Alan Manson came among us like the biggest dog we'd ever seen, and none of us individually had the power to drive him off. If we'd stuck together, we might have managed it. But he rushed in and scattered us, and we were too busy running and sniffing in our own little circles to understand either our strengths or our weaknesses. Agree we did, though, and on a clear summer's night, a week or two after Alan had first appeared to us, we mobilized obediently at the waste ground in preparation for the burning down of Bracey's farmhouse.

Dylan had three containers of petrol hidden in burlap sacks. Alan was pushing a bicycle that had more gallons sloshing hollowly in cans hidden in panniers on either side of its back wheels. Benny and Hedgehog had boxes of kitchen matches and a bunch of oily rags from the garage. Terry had his shorts pockets full of Walnut Whips, one for each of us (except Alan, I was glad to see), which we bit and sucked there on the waste ground before we set out, as if they would bestow on us some kind of knight's courage for the deed ahead.

Alan stood leaning on his bike, smoking one of his inevitable Benson and Hedges. I'd brought nothing, as usual, and neither had Belinda, but I could sense that whereas Alan thought I was worthless, Belinda's presence was all the Walnut Whip he needed. Under the dim light of stars and a first-quarter moon, I watched him watch her as she squirmed her tongue around to get out the last ounce of creamy filling before biting into the whirly chocolate shell.

"Done yet?" Alan asked, in that tone grown-ups use when they're indulging their children almost beyond the limits of patience.

Belinda swallowed hastily. "Ready to go," she said, running her tongue over her teeth to clean them of gunk.

I could hear the crinkle of Walnut Whip wrappers being stuffed into pockets. I covered over the half I hadn't eaten and tucked it away. The chocolate had made me thirsty.

"Okay," Alan whispered into the warm summer almost-dark. "We split up. Me and Belinda and Dylan'll go by the lane."

"Why Belinda?" whispered Terry.

"Twins, you go via the gypsy wood. And Terry and Jay Jalal can get there across the top fields."

"JJ," Dylan said.

"Make sure you stay right by the hedges, you hear me, boys?"

As if Wild Dogs would ever be amateurs enough to show themselves.

"Meet in twenty minutes by the barn at the back of the house," Alan said, and began to wheel his bike over the grass to the lane, Belinda with one hand on the bike's saddle and Dylan lagging some yards behind with his load of sacked petrol. I could tell by the way his head was lowered that he was hating his role as follower.

The remaining four of us looked sheepishly at each other for a moment. Then Benny said, "It's a good plan, you know," and he and Hedgehog loped off down to the wood.

It was a good plan. The trouble was, it wasn't our plan, Dylan's plan. It didn't feel like the usual wacky Wild Dog expedition. Something wasn't right. But while Terry might have been brave enough to say this, braver than I, it seemed too late to say anything at this point, so the two of us just set off like good soldiers everywhere, following orders it was less trouble not to question. We crossed the lane and went through a broken gate into the top fields above Bracey's Farm. It was less dark up on the high ground, the grass like a giant stage lit through a moony gauze, so that we crept around our wings of hedge, with no desire to tread out into centre field, where who knows what hidden audience might burst into noisy, exposing applause. Already, I felt as if the demons of night were at my heels, stalking my clumsy footsteps. Despite the warmth, I had to clench my jaw to stop my teeth chattering.

"The trouble is," I could hear Terry grumbling behind me, "Belinda doesn't see anything except whether people like her or not."

"Shhh," I said, knowing he was right.

"She has to be liked. If someone likes her, she doesn't see anything but that."

"Dylan's with them," I said, trying to keep Terry quiet. I didn't want his worries intruding on my own.

"She used to like Dylan," Terry said. "Until Mr. Big Hound came along."

I stopped walking and turned around, catching Terry by the arms as he bumped into me. "If you don't concentrate," I said, "they'll be there before us, and it'll all be over when we get there."

"JJ . . ." he said and then dropped his eyes.

"Later, okay?" I said.

When Bracey had sold the majority of his land to the developers, he'd kept the farm buildings and several top fields, hoping to throw a protective shield around a place his family had owned since the 1800s. He'd lived on in the farmhouse, surrounded by piles of newly acquired luxuries if you listened to the gossip in the village, until one night he'd died in his sleep.

Vanessa Furse Jackson

And no more than he deserved, went the inevitable local response. Almost immediately, a nephew appeared, who cleared out the contents of the house and stuck up a For Sale sign in the lane outside the farm. But whether, hoping to cash in on his uncle's luck, he was asking too much, or whether the farm was just a bit too far from the village or too run down—who knows?—the For Sale sign was still there three months after it had gone up, and the property was empty of owners. Somehow, Alan had managed to convince us that a strike against the greedy nephew was a strike against the developers, the Avenue dwellers we despised, the ruining of our Wild Dog preserves. We never thought of what his motives might be.

Terry and I were indeed the last to arrive, and the others were already busy carrying straw and sacks from the barn to the house and dropping them through broken windows all around the building. Others besides us had taken advantage of the farm's abandonment, it seemed. Even the back door was half off its hinges. I can still see us quite clearly in my mind, shadowy figures bent double, scuttling like dwarves to and fro across the murky cobbled courtyard, our arms full, our minds intent on our purpose. *Hi ho, hi ho, it's off to work we go.* And Alan standing like some cartoon adult directing our toils, one hand holding a cigarette whose end drew red circles in the dark, the other pointing to where we should go next.

I think now of how many herds of cows must have pattered across that cobbled courtyard to be milked in the great barn, how many teams of Shire horses have clanked their soup-plate feet to a halt and hung patient heads while their harness was unbuckled and heaved off their massive shoulders. How many chickens must have squawked in and out of cart and tractor wheels, how many dogs panted in the shade by the stone water trough— how many daughters, trembling with anticipatory nerves, been escorted out of the yard by fathers in tight Sunday suits to their weddings in the village church where my father had been baptized as a baby.

Sentimentality of that kind is so inseparable from nostalgia that I don't suppose I could have entertained such feelings as a child. But I remember, as I ran submissively back and forth, feeling sick with something more than fear.

When Alan deemed the time ready, he disappeared into the farmhouse with the gallon cans of petrol. Dylan stood next to me in the courtyard, rubbing chaff from his eyes, which must have been smarting as badly as mine were. I could feel the skin on my arms and legs prickling from the dry old straw we'd lugged from barn to house. "Selfish git," Dylan said. "You'd think he was God, the way he carries on."

I had no comfort to offer.

"Painting the signs was much funner," Terry said, from somewhere the other side of Dylan. "Want a Murray mint?" He passed a bag around. The twins came out of the darkness and helped themselves, too. We sucked and waited.

"Where's Belinda?" Terry asked, sounding as if he had at least three sweets in his mouth.

"You and your precious Belinda," Benny said.

Hedgehog grunted.

"I saw her a moment ago," Dylan said. "She's around—don't worry."

How much did Dylan mind, I found myself wondering in the sticky dark, that she now followed Alan as she'd once followed him?

"Okay, troops." Alan loomed out of the back door and beckoned.

We could see Belinda now, hovering just behind him in the doorway. "Watch this," she said, and laughed.

We watched as Alan took a thick Magic Marker out of his pocket and drew a giant, instantly recognizable paw print on the sagging door.

"They're all over the inside of the house," Belinda said, still giggling.

Alan giggled with her. He sounded like Terry. "Give them something to think about," he said. "Yes!" He punched his fist into the dark air a couple of times.

Dylan and I looked at each other and shrugged, but neither of us spoke a word.

Alan pocketed the marker and turned to us briskly. "Okay," he said. "Twins, this side. Dylan, Jalal, Terry round the front. Belinda with me."

"Name's JJ," Dylan muttered under his breath.

I touched his arm in thanks.

"When you hear me whistle," Alan went on, "light matches, as many as it takes, and get them through the windows. Okay? The moment you see a flame, run. And don't stop running till you've reached your homes. Is that clear?"

We nodded owlishly in the dark.

"Okay, okay." Alan's voice was high-pitched, the k's stuttering on the roof of his mouth. "Now go, kids, scram. Go, go, go."

We went. I stood at one front window, Dylan at another, Terry at a third, each of us clutching a box of long kitchen matches. I was shivering and sweating, trails of moisture creeping down the sides of my face like flies, my upper lip slippery, my eyes stinging with chaff and salt. I blinked hard, holding two matches at the ready, as tense as if a guerilla attack were expected to come swarming out of the darkness at any moment.

The low whistle sounded.

I heard Terry squeak with suppressed anxiety. I struck the box with my two matches. Nothing happened. I struck again. Nothing. I threw them through the window, took three out of the box and tried again. They broke. I threw them after the others. I had no sense of what was happening beyond my own failure to carry out orders. I took a reckless bunch of matches from the box and struck them against the side with a great sweep. They exploded into flame, and when I thrust my arm through the window to drop them as far inside as I could, the flame came back out at me, booming into the air and almost knocking me down.

In some mad gesture, I took my half-eaten Walnut Whip out of my pocket and threw it like a sacrificial offering to join the matches in the eager flame. Then I turned and ran around the house, intending to flee home the way I'd come. I ran right into Dylan who clutched a bunch of my T-shirt. "Not that way," he gasped. "By the wood. Darker." We ran at an angle away from the house, trying to locate the track that led into the wood. There was no sign of the twins. I could hear my breath rasping in my throat, could hear Dylan panting, and then I was aware of a third person, whose breaths seemed to come as sobs and little spurts of unintelligible sound. "Shhh," I heard Dylan say, and we stopped for a moment. "Come on," he said. "Come on. Run." But fat Terry was still sobbing for breath and pulling back and, as Dylan held him by one arm, we turned around awkwardly, bumping into each other, to see what he saw.

Clearly silhouetted against the flames leaping out of the old house were Alan and Belinda, he standing with his arms outstretched to the fire, as if in welcome. As we watched, Belinda turned and flung her arms around him. I waited for him to break away as Dylan had done the night of the sign painting, but after a moment he brought his arms in and around her, and then he bent over her in what we all recognized as a classic screen kiss. "Jesus

The Wild Dogs

15

H. Christ," Dylan said, mesmerized, before suddenly finding movement again and dragging Terry on down the track and into the wood. "It's okay, Tel," he said, stopping for a minute and heaving for breath. "Think he wants to get caught? She'll be okay. Come on, run."

And Terry ran, but I could hear him sobbing all the way to the gypsy dump, and when Dylan left us there to climb up to his bungalow, the night beyond the trees bright with fire, he put Terry's sleeve into my hand and told me fiercely that I'd better not let go or else. I didn't let go, and Terry calmed down, probably for lack of breath, and we both got home okay, but I dreamed for months afterwards not about the fire but about running through a dark wood with a huge weight dragging at my right arm and something unspeakable padding after me.

That was how the Wild Dogs came to burn down a small but irreplaceable Queen Anne manor house with an unusual oak-panelled study, an Elizabethan cellar and courtyard, a fifteenth-century barn, and most of Bracey's carefully tended, old-stock apple orchard. Nobody found the paw prints. There was nothing left to find. The hottest, most prolonged summer on record had resulted in perfect conditions for the setting of fires. We could hardly have failed. It was only by the grace of God that we didn't also burn up a tramp who'd been sleeping in the farmhouse for the past few nights. He'd discovered a bottle of whisky the nephew must have overlooked and wandered off with it into the warm night. He was found the next morning, snoring in a ditch by the side of the road, and arrested as a possible suspect. We could have *killed* him—an enormity that, because we hadn't, struck none of us until much later.

Dylan's parents knew he'd been at the fire because they were up and dressed when he got home. Being so close to the farm, they were the first people to dial 999 and were about to go and do what they could to help when he slunk in, stinking of smoke. They didn't beat him—they weren't those sort of parents—but they grieved quietly over him for the rest of the summer, even though he swore, half truthfully, that it wasn't one of his stunts. He said this martyred sorrow was worse than a good beating would have been, which just goes to show how much he knew about beatings.

I had both—the beating and the grieving. My dad caught me climbing back through my bedroom window and didn't wait. He took me down to the store-room and beat me then and there with the leather belt he kept on a nail on the wall for just that purpose. Such was its menace, this hanging tongue of humiliation, that he'd only used it three or four times in my life before this, its presence enough to ensure that I'd never cross any lines he drew—or never get caught crossing them anyway. This time was different. He'd heard the fire engines clangle past. He'd seen the distant light of fire in the sky. He smelled the smoke on me the moment he opened my bedroom door and caught me with one foot still outside the window. He didn't ask what I'd done. He never asked me, even later, where I'd been and what I knew. He beat me because of his own fear, his anger that the police might come into the shop and accuse him of begetting a half-caste criminal for a son. He didn't put on the light in the store-room, just thrashed me there in the dark, careless of where the belt fell. I'll bet he didn't even look down at myself crouched at his feet, sobbing in pain and repentance. It was after that night that I began noticing how little he ever did with me, father and son together. In some indefinable way, I'd become disjoined from him, separated. I was *other*.

My mother didn't try to stop him. Perhaps she felt the administering of justice was his role, his patriarchal right. Perhaps it was. She shook her head sorrowfully over the dark marks left by the belt, smeared ointment on the bruises, and sat by my bed with her hand on my forehead till my even breathing fooled her that I was asleep. How could I sleep when I knew from behind my closed eyelids that she was weeping for me? Among the marks the belt had left, she never noticed the burn on my upper arm that throbbed and smarted through what remained of the night. When she left, I wept, too, overcome by a loneliness that weighted the dark air around me like a smothering blanket.

Neither Dylan's nor my parents breathed a word to anyone else. So by their silences they protected us, as parents do and perhaps should not, preferring their own sentences to the interfering ministrations of courts and outsiders. On the surface, we got away with it. But we weren't innocent, and I knew that. So did Dylan. Terry was consumed by Alan's perfidy, though I don't know how much was guilt over the fire, how much was jealousy and fear of Alan's attraction to Belinda—and, indeed, hers to him. I do know that as blue day succeeded blue day, there grew in both Terry and Dylan a burning desire for some kind of revenge on Alan. What they wanted, as far as I could gather, was to depose him from the position he'd assumed with such insulting ease, to expose a fault line within him that their instincts suggested must be there, even if they had only the haziest idea of what it might be or mean.

"It has to be something he'd really hate," Dylan said, scratching in the powdery earth with a small stick.

He and Terry and I were sitting at the top of the field just below his parents' bungalow a week or so after the burning, and the smell of goat shit was strong on the hot still air.

"Have a sherbet lemon," Terry said, pulling a handful from his pocket.

I didn't feel like one and shook my head. I hadn't felt like much of anything since the fire.

Dylan put his stick down, unwrapped a sweet with care and slid it into the side of his mouth. "Something that'd make him feel looked at," he said, articulating with some difficulty.

"And small," Terry said. "Very small." He unwrapped two sherbet lemons and popped them into his mouth.

They sucked for a bit, then Dylan crunched, and I imagined the tart sherbet escaping the hard lemon outside and making his saliva run. My right arm ached where it had got burned in the fire, and I cradled my elbow with my left hand.

Dylan resumed scratching in the dirt. "He thinks he's such a hot shot," he said. "He's just a dirty old man."

"Belinda goes for walks with him," Terry said morosely. "She won't talk to me about anything else. It's all Alan this and Alan that. I think she's lost her marbles."

The Wild Dogs seemed defunct. All that was left of them was Dylan, Terry and me, sitting here in the fierce heat trying to think how to bring down the Goliath who'd ensured our break-up by the mess he'd got us into. Benny and Hedgehog had hooted with derisive laughter when we'd tried suggesting that what we'd done wasn't just wrong but, in ways we couldn't explain, *bad*.

One of that summer's songs had been yet another re-issue of the Shangri Las' schlocky tear-jerker, "Leader of the Pack," which we publicly despised but secretly listened to when we could indulge its sugary tragedy on our own. I thought of it, sitting in the field with my aching arm, and the words crooned in my head—"As he drove away on that rainy night / I begged him

Vanessa Furse Jackson

to go slow. . . " For want of anything else to contribute, I said, "Perhaps she'll reject him, and he'll drive off into the rainy night and get killed."

The others looked at me as if I'd gone completely loopy.

"'Leader of the Pack,'" I said feebly.

Dylan made barfing sounds. "Get serious, JJ." He scratched at his bit of ground for a while. "Anyway, there hasn't been any rain for weeks."

"Yes, but he's right," Terry said, scrunching around his words. "Alan always has to be leader—in charge, bossing us all around." He sucked in a big slurp of sherbety spit. "We have to knock him down. Ker-pow! Splat!"

"I *know* that," Dylan groaned. "But how?"

"What about if you told your mum about him—you know—kissing Belinda?" I suggested to Terry.

Terry shook his head. "I'd have to say when I saw them," he said. "Otherwise Belinda'd just call me a liar. She'll call me a liar anyway. Or she'll tell Mum where we all were that night. Trust me. She would."

"And that's not enough," Dylan said. "Not just a kiss."

"You don't think anything more happens on their walks, do you?" Terry asked, alarmed. "Do you think I should follow them and see?"

"Maybe it does," Dylan said. "Who knows?"

We sat and thought about it for a while, none of us knowing exactly what *more* might mean, but all of us, I'm guessing, remembering the time we'd seen the Billy goat heave himself onto a nanny outside the bungalow and bring her to her knees before Dylan's mum came in and chased us away from our giggling perch at the window. The Billy had pale rinsed eyes a bit like Alan's, I thought.

"Well, we have to stop it happening, that's all," Dylan said.

My arm throbbed, and I peeked up the sleeve of my T-shirt. The streaky bit looked bigger than it had. It hurt.

"But she's thirteen," said Terry, the teenage state still seeming unattainable to us. She'd had her birthday a week ago, two days after the fire, and neither Dylan nor I had been allowed by our parents to go to see *Bugsy Malone* at the Odeon with the rest of her friends.

"I don't mean stop her, you wally. I mean, stop him," Dylan said, spinning his stick round and round in the dry dirt as if he were trying to start a fire with it.

I looked down the slope of the field to the gypsy wood and its hidden dump below. Everything shimmered and jumped in the heat, and I shut my eyes against the glare.

"Stop him how?" Terry urged.

"Tell everyone he's a perv," I said without thought, my eyes still shut.

"Oh my God," Dylan said, slowly. "You're bloody brilliant, JJ. Of course."

I opened my eyes carefully. "Of course what?"

"Tell them he's a pervert."

"He's what?" Terry asked.

"But not with her. With us," said Dylan triumphantly.

When I got home that afternoon, I was burning with fever. I walked into the shop hardly able to keep my eyes open for the aching weight of their lids, and I stood beside my mother at the till, feeling as if the shelves behind her were reaching arms down out of the shadows to hurt me—or to hold me up—I wasn't sure which. Then I was in the bathroom upstairs being sick. Then I was in my bed, and my heart was beating in my arm, and my mother was stroking my forehead and murmuring, or was she singing to me, as she did when I was very small? I used to understand the language in which she sang, but already, by the time I was ten, the words were fading from my consciousness—my need for acceptance in the narrow world I lived in challenging her desire to keep a part of me among her people. Our people.

When the doctor came, he tsked and tutted and squeezed the brown pus from my arm into a little enamel bowl. There was a needle that smelled like his surgery and stung like a wasp, and there was ointment and a bandage, and there was a deeper sleep than any I'd had since we burned down Bracey's farm. And somewhere in the muddle of time that happened then, there was a long talk with my mother, during which a weeping of guilt and sorrow oozed out as painfully as the pus and brought something of the same relief.

And so it was that I missed taking part in the Wild Dogs' revenge on Alan Manson—or counterattack, as Dylan called it when he sat hugging his knees on the end of my bed and told me what he and Terry had done.

"When two pack leaders fight for dominance," Dylan said, "the smaller of the two has to use cunning, or the bigger one will tear him to pieces."

I still felt a little as if I were floating just above my bed. It was a comfortable feeling, cool and airy. "You were cunning?" I asked.

"Terry and me did it on the same evening," Dylan said, his bare toes

Vanessa Furse Jackson

curling up from my white sheet, so that I could see the small smudges of dirt he'd left there. "The same evening at the same time—we synchronized our watches. We made a pact. Terry's a good guy."

"What did you do?" I asked, as I knew I must.

"We told our parents about Alan, of course," Dylan said.

I leaned back on my pillows. I could sense Dylan was enjoying being able to tell his tale to a brother Dog, so I didn't try and hurry him. "And you said . . . ?"

"We said"—Dylan lowered his voice to a hoarse whisper—"that he'd touched us." He looked at me, his blue eyes as bright and alert as a terrier's.

"Touched you how?" I asked.

"Touched us—all of us—*inappropriately*."

I was slow to pick up on this revelation. "What does that mean?"

"Oh JJ," he said in exasperation and perhaps a bit of embarrassment at having to explain. "Instead of Belinda—you know—him kissing her and that."

"You said that he kissed you?" I asked in mild disbelief.

"No. No, not exactly." Dylan ducked his head and rocked back and forth. "That he touched us. Like on our dicks and so on. You know."

I didn't know exactly, but I saw straight away the brilliance of the strategy. My father had given me a red-faced lecture on the criminality of boys even thinking of other boys *in that way*, and I was aware that in the grown-up world there was no greater sin than men thinking of boys *in that way*, so all in all I reckoned Alan's goose was pretty well cooked. "But you don't want everyone to know, do you?" I said. "I mean you don't want to have to tell other people that he touched you. Even if he didn't. I mean, he didn't. But if he did, you wouldn't want to actually talk about it, would you?"

"That's our genius," said Dylan, crinkling the bright eyes. "Terry and me swore our parents to secrecy. We made them promise we wouldn't have to tell anyone else what happened."

"Then, I don't see . . ." I began.

"Oh, JJ, do hurry up and get better, wool-head," Dylan said, kneeling up in his excitement. "Of course they'll tell people. They'll say they're doing it to protect other kids from him. They'll tell one person at a time in private. It'll go round the village like Chinese Whispers, getting better each time it's passed on, you just wait and see."

So I waited.

For a while, things just seemed to go on much as they had. My arm got well, and I started to go out with Dylan and Terry again, though my mother made me come home much earlier than she used to, and they put a lock on my bedroom window so it would only open a couple of inches. "Too bloody bad if you get hot at night," my dad said. "I want no one coming in or out, you hear me?" Benny and Hedgehog sometimes joined us for a cigarette at the gypsy dump, though we didn't plan any more stunts with them. Belinda told Terry she was tired of hanging out with kids, thank you very much, and I can't say I minded, but I sometimes thought Dylan looked around for her, as if, even unconsciously, he thought she might change her mind and come back.

And then we heard that Alan Manson had died. Been killed only about a month after his parents sold Sea Drift and moved away. The drought of that record hot summer ended with the wettest September the British Isles had experienced since 1918, and there was widespread flooding. Alan died one night in a pile-up on the M4 near Maidenhead during a particularly severe thunderstorm. One car skidded into the pilings of an overpass, and twenty others were unable to brake their way out of trouble. Dylan said the first car was Alan's and it wasn't a skid, but he didn't *know* that.

I maintained it was an accident—I still maintain that. It made me realize, however, just how easily death can come to us, and I became afraid of who it might come to next. In my mind, I saw a brown and swollen river, careening between its banks like the oiled muscles of a snake. I thought how unforgiving and how slippery are the currents by which one man may be sped past danger to safety while another plunges over the weir into the dark mud from which there is no rising. I tried to explain my fears to my mother one night when I'd woken from a drowning dream, but she said only that God protected us from harm if we honoured him and kept his laws. I was a good boy, she said, and had nothing to fear, nothing at all.

But the tramp had lived and Alan had died, one life casually kept safe while another was flung into death, and I couldn't so easily shrug off the mystery. Who had decided? Had we, in truth, been responsible? We'd assigned him the role of criminal and us the roles not of accomplices but of judge and jury. The good guys. We'd run him out of town. But surely it wasn't us who'd exacted this ultimate revenge? Was it God? Nemesis? Or had Alan been hunted down by the fearful, uncanny figure of Death himself, the ultimate big dog?

I stubbornly insisted to Dylan that Alan's death was an accident, and by doing so I think I robbed him not only of the sweetness of his revenge, but also of its justification, its rightness. I found, when we went back to start the new school year in the rain, that the Wild Dogs had simply ceased to exist, as if they'd been rendered extinct. I missed Dylan with a hungry ache, which I shut down by reading books that took me to other lands and peoples—often my mother's—and at weekends I mostly helped in the shop or stayed in my room by myself. Once, I overheard my mother say to my father, "Jay is too much on his own these days. What should we do?"

And he said only, "He's your son. Do what you like with the boy."

Miss Best and Mr. Marvel

"I saw a thrush this morning," Mr. Marvel said.

"A thrush?" Miss Best exclaimed. "You didn't!"

"I did," Mr. Marvel said, with some satisfaction. "On the bank at the far side of the lawn, hopping about on the grass."

"Looking for snails?"

"And finding one, too," he said. "Bang-banging it on one of the big grey stones by the ornamental bridge."

Miss Best looked out of her window. There were no lawns or ornamental bridges to be seen, just the wide concrete path between her building and the building next to it, which had quite nice brickwork, but no windows. "How fantastic!" she said. "And I was just watching a television show about the disappearance of native birds. Thrushes are getting so rare."

"And house sparrows," added Mr. Marvel.

"Oh, I do hope robins are safe," Miss Best said, anxiously. "I couldn't bear it if robins disappeared."

"Christmas cards would never be the same." Mr. Marvel shook his head. "It doesn't bear thinking of," he said.

They sat there for a moment in silence.

"Still," Miss Best said. "You saw a thrush. We must remember that and rejoice."

Mr. Marvel puffed out his moustache. "Beautiful breast. Quite beautiful. I remember once . . ." His eyes grew dreamy.

Miss Best sighed with pleasure. He'd brought her a story. "Yes?" she breathed.

"It was a summer at Ashenleigh, right at the end of the war," he began.

"I'd brought Ada down to meet my parents. Well, to meet my father, really, I suppose. Ma would have loved anyone who loved me, but the old boy could be prickly—thought all modern girls were light-skirts, only after one thing."

"Your money?" hazarded Miss Best.

"No, no, my honour, my manhood—love you and leave you—that sort of thing." Mr. Marvel looked a bit pink.

"Goodness," said Miss Best. "I thought parents worried about that only if they had daughters. My father wouldn't have any young man in the house after ten p.m."

"Well, Ada was allowed to stay, but she was put in the bedroom next to my parents. Thin walls between. Made it quite a challenge." He cleared his throat. "Anyway, that wasn't what I was remembering."

Miss Best tilted her head to one side, raised an eyebrow.

"Not all I was remembering, damn you, woman."

She laughed. She still had a pretty laugh. "Go on."

"It was one of those gorgeous days that one recollects when one thinks of past summers," Mr. Marvel went on, "but that are, in meteorological fact, comparatively rare. Golden sun, fresh morning, green world, birds singing—you know the kind of thing. It was after breakfast, and Ada and I were sitting on the terrace outside the French windows, looking out over the garden. Only of course my father wouldn't call them French windows after Dunkirk—not very charitable towards the French, my father—refused to eat anything containing garlic or olives for the same reason. He called them the door windows instead."

"Door windows—how very fascinating," said Miss Best, entranced.

"So there we were, Ada and I, sitting on the old wooden seat outside the door windows, looking out over the lawn at those circular rose beds dotted everywhere—big blowzy tea roses, all those reds and yellows floppeting about, you prob'ly know their names. My father never knew the names of anything, but that's what his father'd planted back in 1908 when they bought the place—great one for tradition, my father. So he entrusted the care of the garden to Ma and she left it all to old Jamieson to do. Had a son killed at Arnhem, poor old man, never really regained his strength after the war, but he was a wizard gardener—everything bloomed for him. I always thought those rose-beds looked a bit thorny and unfriendly myself—all that bare earth, if you know what I mean. But the great blooming heads, how pretty they were that day—oh, I can see them now." Mr. Marvel sighed deeply.

"Why after Dunkirk?" asked Miss Best.

"Ha! What? Well, after Dunkirk, you see, Father washed his hands of the French—said it was typical of them to let the devil in and the angels out—wouldn't have any doors in his house called French windows, no, by God. Bit of a Wogs begin at Calais sort of chap, my old dad. Sorry."

"No, no, don't be sorry," said Miss Best. "Go on. You were with Ada on the terrace."

"After breakfast."

"After breakfast, yes. What age would she have been as she sat beside you on the old wooden seat?" Miss Best was there, in the sunshine, on the terrace. She smelled the roses.

"Hmm, let me see, she must have been, yes, she'd just have turned twenty-three. I was a little older, of course—felt I could protect her—little Ada." He cleared his throat.

"Twenty-three," murmured Miss Best, remembering the combs with which she used to sweep back her hair, so it fell in curls behind her ears.

"Well, then," said Mr. Marvel, picking up his tale. "There we were, sitting in the sunshine, full of eggs and bacon and the joys of young love. Holding hands discreetly, ahem, so no one could see from inside the house."

"Fresh eggs, not dried?" asked Miss Best. It was important that the story be historically accurate.

"They had eggs at Ashenleigh all through the war. Rhode Island reds. My mother kept them."

"Your father didn't mind Americans, then?" said Miss Best, twinkling.

"Americans? Oh. Yes, ha! Very good. No, he always said he'd have married Mary Pickford if he hadn't met my mother first. Though he couldn't stand Roosevelt, of course—bolshy socialist pinko, he called him. Bit unfair, I always thought, but there. Where was I?"

"On the terrace," said Miss Best. "I do apologize. The eggs distracted me."

"Holding hands, yes. We had our own pigs, too, by the way. Jamieson dealt with those, though. Lovely animals. I always used to go straight to the sties when I came home on leave. One could lean over the low wall for hours scratching a bristly pink back with a stick—you relaxed, pig relaxed, it was a wonderful way to wind down before tea and questions in the drawing-room."

"From your parents, yes." Miss Best nodded, sympathetically.

"Bit like coming home from school, coming home on leave," said Mr. Marvel. "Same inquisition or so it seemed to me. What have you been doing since we last saw you? Are your superiors pleased with you? When can we expect your promotion? Have you made any nice friends? That sort of thing. Couldn't stand it sometimes."

"You poor man," said Miss Best, with deep sympathy. "Mine was always that last question. Have you made any nice friends? Meaning men friends. Meaning, when are you going to catch yourself a husband and get married? Infuriating when I longed to have what other girls did, wanted so much to love. To be loved. I would have given anything." She stopped, out of breath from the shock of anger that had blown through her.

Mr. Marvel took one of her hands in his and held it gently.

"What they were really asking was why do we have a poor virginal failure for a daughter?" Miss Best took a tissue from a box next to her chair and wiped her eyes. She looked out at the concrete wall and brick path outside. Mr. Doughty was taking his regular afternoon constitutional, leaning heavily on his walker, taking tiny steps on feet he kept so tightly clamped together, it was as if he wore invisible leg-cuffs. I used to be able to do that, thought Miss Best.

"I wouldn't come here if I didn't—well—you know," said Mr. Marvel.

"Like me," said Miss Best and smiled a watery smile. "If you didn't like me. I know."

"Well, I jolly well do," he said. "Now where was I?"

"I like you, too," she said. "I don't know what I would do without you. I know exactly why I named you Mr. Marvel, you dear man." She blew her nose.

Mr. Marvel (and it was true that this was not his real name) whiffled deprecatingly through his moustache. "Well," he said, "with a name like Best, you needed the illusion that I was on your august and elevated level, perhaps. Ha!"

"Such a silly name, Best," she said. "It simply had the effect of making me aware I wasn't." She shifted slightly in her chair.

"Hurting?" he said.

"Go on," said Miss Best. "You were sitting on the old wooden seat on the terrace with Ada. What was she wearing?"

Mr. Marvel thought for a moment. "Good question—what would she have been wearing?"

"Did she have combs in her hair?" asked Miss Best.

"No, no, wait now. She had a straw hat with a wide brim, I remember. Got in the way a bit. And her frock was white, that's it. A white frock with three-quarter length sleeves. What else? A round collar like a blouse, you know. Buttons, I think, some buttons down the front. And a narrow, blue leather belt around her waist. By Jove, yes, it was pretty. That little waist, could put both hands around it, and all that white stuff falling from the line of blue. Fresh as the springtime," he added, originally.

"Made from an old sheet probably," said Miss Best. "Linen, if she was lucky. Or perhaps butter muslin. We had to make do and mend in those days." But in her mind the exquisite Ada was attired in couturier perfection, a vision of the kind of loveliness that Miss Best remembered so well sighing over in dark cinemas. A dream heroine, unsuitably but immaculately dressed and coiffed for every scene.

There was a thumping knock on the door. Miss Best, her mind's film un-spooling, started slightly. Mr. Marvel withdrew his hands tactfully as a nursing aide bustled in with Miss Best's afternoon cup of tea. "Hello, Angel," Mr. Marvel said. "How opportune—just what we need, a nice cup of tea."

"Angela to you," said the woman, tartly.

"'A ministering angel shall my sister be,'" rhapsodized Mr. Marvel, with an expansive sweep of his arms.

"Here you are then, ducks," said Angela to Miss Best. She removed the box of tissues from reach and plunked down the cup of tea on the small table by Miss Best's chair, so that some of the liquid rocked into the saucer. "Need the potty before you drink that, do you, lovie?"

"I do not," Miss Best said, stiffly. "Thank you."

"I suppose you're going to want yours in here, too, aren't you?" Angela said, slipping both her arms under Miss Best's and giving her an expert pull up.

"If it would not be too much trouble," Mr. Marvel said, inclining his head.

"And perhaps a couple of biscuits to go with the tea?" Miss Best added, but her suggestion was made to Angela's retreating back as she whisked out of the room in a haste that clearly signified the trouble to which she was being put.

"Hamlet," said Mr. Marvel.

"That woman," sighed Miss Best.

"About Ophelia. After he'd driven her to kill herself, naturally."

"A ministering angel?" said Miss Best. "That hardly describes Angela." She had needed pulling up in her chair, but her back was protesting at Angela's brisk methods.

"She's in such a hurry, that one, she won't stay around long enough for her own funeral," said Mr. Marvel.

"Well, she won't be missed," said Miss Best with asperity, and the two of them broke into peals of laughter.

There was a frenzied wail from the next-door room. "There they are again. The flies have got in. The flies have got in. Help me. The flies have got in."

"Oh Gawd," said Mr. Marvel. "We've woken up Miss Cuckoo."

"Shhh," said Miss Best. "You mustn't call her that." She put a hand up to her mouth to stifle her laughter.

They listened to Angela go into the room, heard the steady murmur of her voice, and the wailing slowly died down again.

"Poor old thing," said Miss Best.

"We're lucky, you and I," said Mr. Marvel. "We still have our faculties."

"We may not be able to walk," agreed Miss Best, "but at least we can still think."

"Slight loss of legs but all our marbles," said Mr. Marvel, and they were still laughing, though more quietly this time, when Angela returned with a second cup of tea, disapproval radiating from her like disinfectant.

"You'll have to balance it on your lap," she said, handing the cup and saucer to Mr. Marvel. "And mind you don't spill any on your rug. We're much too busy to be cleaning up after you today, so just you be careful, you hear me?"

"Yes, Mummy," said Mr. Marvel.

"Bloody cheek," said Angela as she swept out.

"And no biscuits, of course," said Miss Best.

"I wonder why they work here, these women," said Mr. Marvel, raising his tea and sucking it carefully through his moustache.

Miss Best put both hands around her cup and managed a tremulous sip, but the cup was such an awkward shape and her hands so clumsy today that she put it down again. "Potty, indeed," she said, still outraged that the question should have been asked in front of a gentleman. "Have they no manners?"

"You notice that we may take no liberties," said Mr. Marvel. "Yet we are *ducks* and *lovie* to them."

"Children."

"Children," he agreed.

"Oh dear," said Miss Best. "I've spilt some on my lap." She looked around for a tissue, then dabbed with her thumb. "I shall be in trouble, I suppose."

"Serves the silly cow right for slopping it in the first place," said Mr. Marvel, with sudden viciousness. He drank his tea, fulminating.

"We mustn't complain," Miss Best said, after a pause. Her back ached, and she thought how nice it would be to lie down for a while.

"Why bloody not?"

Miss Best looked over at the corner of her room where stood the enormous hoist with which she was moved from chair to bed. Like some obscene dowager's carriage, she thought, waiting motionless for the horse to be buckled into its slings and harness. By Angela, the coachman with the reins and whip. She chuckled at the picture then looked over at her friend.

He glanced up from his cup, caught her eye, and smiled unwillingly. "All right, all right," he said. "No complaining. No point anyway. No damn point." He leaned sideways with some difficulty and set his cup and saucer down on the floor with a clatter. "That'll give her something to suck her teeth about," he said with satisfaction. "Now, where was I?"

"On the terrace," said Miss Best. "On the old wooden seat, with Ada." She shut her eyes to retrieve the picture. "Who is in a white dress with a blue belt and a cartwheel straw hat with long blue ribbons. Her eyes match the belt and the ribbons, and her lips are the colour of the red roses at which she is looking."

"By Jove," said Mr. Marvel. "You're absolutely right. Blue ribbons on the hat, yes, I'd forgotten that."

"Ada is twenty-three and quite lovely," Miss Best went on. "She is also very much in love with you."

Vanessa Furse Jackson

"Very much in love," he repeated. "Yes."

"Are you about to propose, by any chance?" asked Miss Best, delicately.

"Ah," said Mr. Marvel. He rested his elbows on the arms of his chair, brought his hands together in a praying shape, and rested his chin on the tips of his fingers. "I was just getting to that." He thought for a moment, his brow furrowed.

"Are you in uniform?" Miss Best asked, giving him time to collect himself.

"No, I am not in uniform." He corrected himself. "I was not in uniform. Wouldn't have done to wear it around the house, you know. I was in a pair of pre-war flannels, unfashionably wide, white shirt, no tie."

"And a cricketing jersey?" suggested Miss Best.

"Too warm. Sleeves rolled up. Jacket hung over the arm of the seat, that kind of thing."

"All right," said Miss Best. "Carry on."

"It was the thrush that got me started," Mr. Marvel said. "Seeing that thrush this morning. There were thrushes at Ashenleigh, too, many, oh many thrushes."

"On the lawn that morning?"

"On the lawn that very morning! Questing in the earth beneath the rose bushes, bringing their snails to the bottom of the terrace and breaking the shells on the stone steps there."

"And singing that wonderful, glittering song from the surrounding trees," said Miss Best.

"Alas, I don't remember that," Mr. Marvel said. "But I do remember my father on the subject."

"Elms and limes and willows and a great spreading cedar of Lebanon," said Miss Best, rapt.

"Called 'em those damned Frog birds. Frog birds because they ate snails, you see." Mr. Marvel raised up his head and guffawed with laughter. "Frog birds, oh lordy."

Miss Best opened her eyes. "You're not concentrating," she said.

Mr. Marvel wiped his eyes. "Sorry," he said. "Sorry. Lost my train of thought there for a moment."

"The thrushes are questing. The smell of roses is overpowering. You are about to propose," said Miss Best, closing her eyes again.

"I couldn't go down on one knee or anything," said Mr. Marvel. "Because of the possibility that we were being overlooked from behind the door windows. I couldn't even turn to her properly because of that damned hat she had on. So I clasped her hands a little tighter in mine, and I think she knew I was about to speak."

"Yes," whispered Miss Best.

"Would you do me the honour?"

"Yes?"

"The honour of becoming my wife?"

"Yes, oh yes."

"That's exactly right—exactly what she did say. No need for anything else, you see."

"How wonderful!"

"I was bold enough to lift her hands to my lips. I was overcome, quite overcome."

"I understand completely."

"No more words. So I reached over to my jacket pocket and got out my cigarette case—gave us both one, and we lit up and sat there in the sunshine smoking. Oh, those were the days," said Mr. Marvel, with longing in his voice.

Miss Best had never smoked. "Cigarettes?" she said. "At a moment like this?" She opened her eyes and looked over at Mr. Marvel.

He caught her glance, guiltily, then rallied. "At that very moment," he cried, "my father came lunging through the door windows like a rogue elephant in must, galloped around the old wooden seat, and stood before Ada and me gobbling like a turkey in his incoherent rage."

"Either an elephant or a turkey. Not both, surely?" said Miss Best.

"Trumpeting and gobbling his displeasure," continued Mr. Marvel, magnificently. "I could feel Ada's little hands trembling in mine."

"Where are the cigarettes?" hissed Miss Best.

"We had pitched our cigarettes over the front of the terrace at the first sound of movement from within."

"I hope you didn't hit any thrushes," said Miss Best, but she was thrilled nevertheless. "And then?" she urged.

"And then," said Mr. Marvel, "before he could get a word in edgeways, I stood up (I was taller than he) and, looking down at him, said quietly but

Vanessa Furse Jackson

firmly, 'Father, I would like to present to you my fiancée. Ada has done me the honour of accepting my hand in marriage.'"

"Bravo!" exclaimed Miss Best.

"That was it," said Mr. Marvel. "The poor old boy caved in immediately, still red in the face and sputtering, but quite defeated. Bowed before her. Kissed her hand."

"Oh, how marvellous," said Miss Best. "How marvellous." She closed her eyes and leaned back into her chair.

"It was rather, wasn't it?" said Mr. Marvel. "A damned good story, though I say it as shouldn't."

Miss Best smiled. "Mmm," she murmured, contentedly.

"You're tired, dear lady. Time for me to be taking myself off. What a pleasure this has been. Many thanks for putting up with me."

Miss Best tried to beg him to stay longer, but she was indeed tired. It was almost time for the dowager's carriage. "Thank *you*, dear friend," she said. "I don't know what I would do without you."

Mr. Marvel leaned forward, took one of her swollen, twisted hands in his, and kissed it gallantly, as he always did before leaving. "Till next time, then, my beauty," he said, and took the brake off his chair. Reversing carefully, he felt a wheel run over something hard. There was a jolt, a loud crack, and "Oh damn," said Mr. Marvel. "I've just run over the cup and saucer."

The two friends looked at each other in consternation. He sighed and then shrugged. "No use crying over spilt china," he said. "I'll tell them as I go past the nursing station."

"That'll be the last cup of tea you'll ever get from Angela," said Miss Best.

He rolled his wheelchair backwards to the doorway. "Goodbye my dear Miss Best," he said.

"Goodbye Mr. Marvel," said Miss Best. "Come back soon. I want to hear all your stories, and we don't have much time, do we?"

Mr. Marvel spun his chair around expertly in the wide corridor. "We have the rest of our lives," he said, and he laughed—a boy's laugh—as he rolled away, rubber wheels squeaking on the polished linoleum.

Miss Best laid her head back in her chair and closed her eyes. Beginning to drift into sleep, she was dimly aware of song glittering through the great spreading cedar above the scent of roses and, farther off, of the bumbling, narcotic buzzing of a trapped fly.

Rain

Outside the window, all she could see was a grey and white impression of the February garden, the grass grey, the end-wall grey, the graveyard beyond the garden increasingly out of focus as it flattened towards the dissolving horizon. Bella sighed, pushed in the eco-save button on the dishwasher, and leaned forward, squinting over the sink in a vain effort to clear the view from grey to green. But the window was fogged from the heat in the kitchen, as if the inside was in league with the outside.

"What are you doing?" asked Jonathan, popping his head around the door.

"Clearing up the kitchen," Bella snapped. "What does it look as if I'm doing?"

The dishwasher sighed into action like an obedient dog unwillingly roused from slumber.

"That was a good lunch, Bella, thanks."

She didn't answer him, intent on wringing out her dishcloth into the sink.

"Bella, don't be mad at me," Jonathan coaxed from the doorway.

She wiped the taps, the surrounds of the sink, the white tiled counter-top.

"I promised I'd get this job delivered first thing Monday morning," he went on. "But I'll think up something fun for us to do tonight, okay?"

As if I was a child to be placated, Bella thought.

"Bella?"

She stared out of the window, concentrating on blocking him from her mind. Was rain actually falling, she asked herself carefully, or was the familiar world merely diffracted with mist? Nice word, *diffracted*.

If Bella had been outside, she would have known it was raining—raining quite hard, in fact—but in those fine skeins that fall from the air in spiralling threads, netting your hair and face, seeping down the back of your neck, filling your shoes with wet sky.

Ben Wilkins wouldn't have put it quite like that.

Fuckin' rain, he was grumbling to himself. On top of everything else. You'd of thought it could lay off, just for once. Could of waited till I were done. Fuckin' rain, always raining. Jesus.

He peered down again, forgetting to hold up the flowers he was carrying. "*Shit*," he said, as the plastic wrapping scraped along the sodden ground.

Sorry Carrie, wash my mouth out. Can't see a fuckin' thing, can I?

He straightened his back with some difficulty, walked on five paces, and bent down again, careful to keep his left arm up this time. Where are you, then, Carrie?

A little dog trotted up to him and stood at his heel.

"Where's Carrie, then, Joe?"

A fox terrier, brown and white, bright of eye and impervious to rain.

"Go seek her then, boy."

Joe sat down on neat haunches, his tongue out. "Fat lot of good you are," Ben said.

When Bella turned around, Jonathan had faded away, as she had known he would. He didn't like moods. He would have gone to his studio and switched on the music for the afternoon, assuring himself that it would be much better just to leave her alone. There wasn't, she had once told him, an empathetic bone in his body. "Just as well," he'd said cheerfully. "If I felt how you feel every time you feel like you're feeling now, we'd both have gone down to the river and jumped in long ago." And she'd laughed, but with resentment, longing as she always did for the hug he wouldn't give her until she promised him she felt better.

She hung the cloth over the sink to dry. Going to the door, she turned off the flat glare of the fluorescent lights and looked back for a moment at the kitchen window, smaller now in the shadowy room, the square of grey outside both lighter and less discernable. She crossed the hall, Miles Davis blowing his repeated, mournful *So What* from behind a door she mustn't open, and went upstairs to the bedroom.

Vanessa Furse Jackson

Outside in the graveyard, the raindrops beaded on the wire curls over Joe's shoulders and down his spine, and every so often he shook them off violently, water springing in an arc around him, coiling a thong of spray around Ben's knees. "Goddamit, dog," Ben would yelp, shaking each sopping leg far less effectually than Joe. "How much wetter do I need to get? Keep your rain to yourself, mate, you hear me?"

And Joe would put his nose to the ground and trot off into the murk, stump of a tail up like an antenna seeking a good reception.

Ben's back was aching, his wet knees were aching, and his raincoat was soaked around the hem and the upturned collar. His tweed cap was furred with moisture like Joe's coat, an efficient protection for his head but not for his ears or neck, both of which felt as if the coldness of the rain had worked itself deep under the skin.

I could of sworn it was up here, he said to himself. Main entrance over there, yews by the gate, row of posh houses behind the wall.

"Forget your own head next, you will," Carrie had said to him once, probably more than once, but he remembered this time because he'd got it right for a change.

"Not me, girl," he'd said to her. "My head's screwed on tight enough. It's just that I don't always remember the unimportant things any more. Ain't got room for everything. So what?"

He could hear her now. "Ain't got room? Ben Wilkins, you got nothing *but* room in that big head of yours. It's all air from ear to ear."

"'Ere to where?" Ben had said, plaintively he hoped.

"Ears, I said, cloth-head. Between your ears. And how do you know what's important and what's not? Answer me that!"

And he'd said to her what he usually found too difficult to say. "I love you, Carrie. That's important. I know that, don't I? So what's else to remember?"

"Oh Ben," Carrie had said, with that look. "Oh Ben."

It's all very well to Oh Ben me, he grumbled now, ignoring the look as best he could for its being imprinted on his mind like a photograph. But I feel a right Charlie out here in the fuckin' rain when it *is* important and I can't bloody *find* it.

Bella stood at the bedroom window and watched the raindrops spring lightly onto the glass outside, then gather weight until they overflowed into little streams that strengthened as they fell. Her chest felt tight, as if not quite enough air was reaching her lungs.

How can you tell me not to feel like this when I do feel like this? she asked the absent Jonathan. I can't not feel something just because you'd rather I didn't. I can't unfeel.

She rubbed a finger against the window-pane, as if to prove that she couldn't affect the melancholy of the rain. She stared at her reflection, blurred and disfigured by the water that was flowing down the glass as if it would never stop.

Work, always work. What about me? It's Sunday afternoon and you're still working, always in your precious studio, leaving me alone. Again.

"You're never alone," Jonathan had said to her, in one of those conversations she was angry to discover she could not erase from memory. "Look around you, use your eyes. There's always something to explore, to store up for later. Something or someone."

"But I don't want something or someone," she had protested. "I only want *you*. And you're not here." Why did love bring with it such anguish?

"I *am* here," Jonathan said, touching her between her breasts. "I will always be here. But so is the rest of the world. Go out, Bellissima. Go out and look at it for yourself."

And she had shut her eyes and pressed herself into his arms, against his warm body, as if she could climb inside his skin.

Go out, go out, she mouthed to her rain-ghost in the glass. Why don't you go out, you smug bastard? Get out of your nice warm studio and look for me. *Me*.

Ben whistled into the afternoon gloom, and Joe appeared from behind a slab of granite, his muzzle choked with earth, his tongue dripping saliva and mud.

"'Ere," Ben said in alarm. "You ain't digging anything up in this place, are you?"

Joe shook himself.

"Where's Carrie, then, Joe? Go seek. Good dog, go seek!"

But it was only her voice that came to him, sounding down from her bedroom window when he was out in the garden hoeing between young cabbages and sprouts. When he was breathing clean air away from the sickroom for a while, if he was honest.

Vanessa Furse Jackson

"Benjamin Wilkins, it's high time you came in out of that rain and had a nice cup of tea. You'll catch your death out there."

"I know, I know, don't nag, woman."

"I'm not nagging, you old coot. I'm looking after your stubborn self, not that you deserve it. Now get on in before I have to come out there and drag you in myself."

"Shut the bloody window, Carrie. I'll come when I've finished going down this row and not before."

"You obstinate old man."

"You beautiful pussycat, you gorgeous sexy bosom, you."

"Oh Ben."

God damn it, where *is* it? I'm going to catch my death if I'm not careful.

Bella listened. Downstairs, the dishwasher hiccupped, stopped, began its soft, swishing breaths again. Across its rhythm, Miles thrummed faintly, his trumpet flying above the band, though she couldn't make out which track was now playing. She brought her senses back into the bedroom and began to hear the undercurrent of rain— a soughing through the cypress in the next-door garden, a muted, irregular riffle against the window, a steady pat pat as it collected and fell to the ground from her window-sill.

She opened the bottom of the sash window to hear better and breathed in a great gulp of grey air, closing her eyes against the galvanizing chill of it. She breathed out in a great whoosh, breathed in again, opened her eyes.

There was an old man walking in the graveyard. Wandering slowly, reading headstones. No one else around at all.

She'd never been into the graveyard, repulsed in a way she didn't care to examine by what it contained. But now, the winding paths, the clusters of trees and bushes, even the huddled gravestones suddenly seemed inviting. The pearly green rain softened outlines, promising her a solitude not of the shut-out-of-the-room kind but welcoming and inclusive. She took another stinging breath.

Summoned into energy, she turned from the window, grabbed a sweater, and plummeted downstairs. She found her sturdy red boots and her pink gore-tex jacket in the scrum of the hall cupboard, and was out of the front door and halfway down the street before she thought of telling Jonathan where she was going. As if he'd even care, she said savagely to herself, zipping the jacket up round her neck and pulling the hood tight over her head. She began to run, released for the moment, buoyant.

She ran to the end of the road, turned right into Cemetery Lane, and then walked beside the high grey wall until she reached the iron gates, open, said the discreet black and gold notice, until 6.00 pm. Once inside, she slowed, blinking at the flurries of rain from which the wall had partially protected her and also at the sudden rush of space. It was, she thought, as if the grimy, car-crammed streets outside had been taken up and shaken out like a clean sheet, all wrinkles sliding away to leave a great aerated tent of opalescent light. *Opalescent*, she mouthed, tasting the sounds and the rain on her tongue. She stood still, alive to the wet-scented air and the thick quality of the silence that is peculiar to damp winter days and secret places in cities. She drew in another breath, held it until her blood had warmed it, then expelled its visible shape out before her. She began walking back along the inside of the wall. When she reached the edge of the cemetery, she turned left along the lower wall that separated it from the row of houses in which she lived.

From some distance away, Ben watched her, sourly resenting the intrusion of another person into a place he'd had to himself till now. Silly cow, he said to himself. Just look at her, blimey. Bright pink jacket, tight jeans, daft little shiny scarlet bootee things, and she thinks she's dressed for the weather. He pulled his cap down and the collar of his grey raincoat up around his cold ears, and sniffed. He cleared his throat, spat, and turned his back on the intruder. "'Ere, Joe," he called softly. "Stay close, mate—foreign bodies about." Rounding a stone angel, Joe lifted his leg on a wing, trotted up to Ben, and shook himself violently. "*Fuckin'* rain," said Ben and bent down to his task again.

Funny seeing the house from the back like this, Bella thought, looking up at the top half of it, which was all she could see over the garden wall. Lots of angled drain pipes, window frames that needed painting, bits of dead creeper, a plastic bag stuck in the gutter. Like catching your mother in her underwear. Not so intrusive if it was a stranger but made awkward because of intimacy. Oh damn, and I left the bedroom window open and the precious Paloma curtains are blowing out into the rain.

There was a gravel path almost opposite where she was standing that led away from the row of houses and towards the middle of the graveyard.

Vanessa Furse Jackson

Bella walked onto it, then turned and began to back down it, watching her made-strange house slowly stretch up above the wall as she got farther from it. Jonathan had gone into the cemetery when they first moved here six months ago, but it wasn't very interesting, he told her—mostly Victorian and later, with nobody of note buried here—so except for being grateful for the green space behind the house, they'd ignored its presence. Perhaps we never explore what's closest to us, she thought. It's just there, so we go somewhere else. She didn't acknowledge the unease she'd felt about the graveyard's purpose, which anyway seemed to have subsided in the face of its physical thereness She hugged to herself the moist air, the rain outside her pink hood, the unmapped terrain that lay right next to her safe house and that this afternoon she had all to herself.

"Don't look round, Joe, but that daft biddy's walking backwards," Ben said. "Jesus, why can't she just piss off and leave us alone?" He abandoned the row of stones he was examining and turned down another path that curved around a cluster of laurels, until his view of the intruder was blocked by a busily ornate mausoleum encased in iron railings. He leaned back against the railings and closed his eyes for a moment.

Eventually, Bella began to feel a little dizzy from walking backwards and turned around to see where she was. The grass on either side of the path was ragged and dingy, but the lettering on the gravestones seemed sharply focused by the wet. Bella bent down to them. Here Lies Peter Parrilees, Sometime Councillor of this Parish, she read. Parrilees, heavens. In Memory of Our Beloved Mother, Edna May, Wife of Alfred George Sparkton, At Last Peace from the Travails of this World, R.I.P. *Hic Jacet* Rose Joycelyn Markham, Jan 23rd to Jan 25th, 1926. How sad. In Proud Memory of Squadron Leader Algernon "Bulgy" Barnes, D.F.C., 24th July, 1940, Returning to the Sky with Wings.

It was still misting with rain and very quiet. Bella climbed up from the squeaky gravel path to the muting grass and wandered at random among the stone crosses and shields, the cherubs and praying hands, the plain, uncompromising slabs, the slime of old chrysanthemums and the little pointy snouts of early snowdrops just showing above the ground. She felt at one with herself, peaceful. She looked, she touched but was for the moment untouched by the melancholy that can hang like low cloud over such places on winter afternoons. Once, coming to another path, she found a bouquet of white lilies and carnations, still sheathed in florists' wrapping, lying on the gravel. It seemed a shame to leave them dying there, so she picked them up and carried them with her, thinking that somewhere there would be a grave where she would know to leave them.

Ben counted to a hundred then deemed it safe to leave the shelter of the mausoleum. Peeling himself off its wet railing, he went back along the curving path to resume his search.

He heard her before he saw her.

"What are you doing, little dog-person? Are you all by yourself, then? Aren't you sweet?"

Oh *shit!* he thought.

"You're all wet, baby paws. Look at you."

And there was Joe, shamelessly playing the abandoned stray, stump wagging, ears flattened pathetically, muzzle lifted in supplication.

"Enough to make a worm puke, you are," Ben said.

"Oh, I'm sorry," said Bella, getting to her feet in a hurry.

"Not you, him." Ben nodded toward Joe. "Baby Paws over there."

There was a moment's silence, during which Joe looked at neither of them but began to lick a shoulder with deep concentration.

"He's a lovely dog," Bella said.

"He's all right, Joe is," Ben said.

There was another silence, which might have led to the awkward moves of strangers parting had not Ben suddenly noticed what Bella was carrying. "The flowers," he said. "Blimey, where'd I leave those, then?"

"Oh, are they yours?" Bella asked.

"Forget my own head next," Ben said.

"I found them on one of the paths back there," Bella said. "I'm not sure which one, I'm afraid. I was wandering rather. But not far away. I expect I could find it if it's important."

"No, it's not the path I've lost," Ben said. "Though I'm grateful to you for picking up the flowers, Miss. Thank you."

"Bella," she said, handing him the bouquet.

"That means beautiful, don't it?" he said, taking the flowers from her rather awkwardly.

"It's my name. Arabella, actually, only that's such a mouthful."

"Benjamin Wilkins."

Vanessa Furse Jackson

They shook hands gravely over the faint sweet smell of lilies.

"Pleased to meet you, Mr. Wilkins," Bella said. She realized that this was true, so she smiled at him.

"You could call me Ben," he said and cleared his throat.

"Ben," she repeated, adding, "Have you lost something else, then?"

"Something else?"

"You said it wasn't the path you'd lost."

"Oh that. No," he said. "It's Carrie I can't find. I've looked all over for her."

Bella looked at him with concern. "There's no one here besides us," she said. "And Joe. I was looking down at the place from my bedroom window before I came out, and I did catch a glimpse of you. But no one else. See over there?" She pointed back towards the row of houses. "That's my house—the one with the curtains blowing out of the window."

"Get wet, those will," Ben said absently.

"I know," she said. "Jonathan's going to be absolutely livid if he finds out I was so stupid."

"Well, I won't tell a soul," Ben said, and smiled. "Carrie would of tore my head off if I'd done something like that."

Bella waited.

"Carrie's my wife," Ben said. "She's buried here somewhere, only I can't find the grave, see?"

"Oh, I *am* sorry," Bella said.

"Don't be sorry. It's my own bloody fault for not taking better note at the funeral. I could of sworn I'd remember. But she's right. I do forget important things and that's a fact."

"No," Bella said. "I meant I'm sorry she's dead."

"We came up on the train," Ben said. "Me and Joe. It's been a year, see? I bought the flowers at Victoria Station. Then we took a bus. I remembered that bit all right—found the place and all. But now I can't find Carrie."

The thin rain was still coming down, but Bella was afraid to look at Ben in case she saw tears on his face as well. She averted her gaze and watched Joe quietly wander off, nose questing in the damp grass.

"You'll be thinking I should have come before this," Ben went on. "But I promised her, see? Once a year, she said, and that's quite enough. You save your money, she said, for what's important, and no hanging round my grave, you hear me? She wanted to be buried with her ma and pa, and I carried out her wishes to the last. Today's the anniversary and here I am. But it's a long way from Lewes, Miss. Bella, I should say. On a train with Joe, though he's ever so good and lies under my feet with no fuss. A long way on a pension." His voice sounded uncertain. "And it's after three o'clock."

"You know," Bella said, a disturbing picture in her mind of the old man wandering around the cemetery in the dark while she lay with Jonathan under their goose-down duvet, making love to the soothing music of rain outside the window. "You know, I'm thinking that the newer graves are closer to the entrance I came in at this afternoon. Closer to the row of houses where I live, I mean. I'm sure I noticed more recent dates along the wall there, and more flowers and things."

Ben lifted up the lilies and carnations as if to a distant trumpet. "Well, lead on, girl," he said. "What are we waiting for?"

Bella found herself praying to a half-forgotten God that her instincts and memory were right. As she wound her way back to the boundary wall, with Ben following her and Joe trotting ahead, she was chanting in her mind, Please find Carrie for us, please find her, please, please find her. Her desire to help Ben was so urgent she could feel it as a physical constriction in her chest.

As they came up the path she'd backed down earlier and got closer to the garden wall, she began to fear she would fail. All the graves they passed appeared equally crumbling and blurred, and the incantation in her mind seemed increasingly meaningless. But it was there after all, a low, pale stone glowing in the dull air, its lettering blade-sharp: *In Memory of Carol Susan Wilkins, Beloved Wife of Benjamin, Never Forgotten.*

"And right over there's her ma and pa, just as she wanted," said Ben.

Bella sighed with thankfulness. "Oh, Ben, isn't that lovely?" she said, meaning that her prayer had been answered but also, in some comforting, unexamined way, that Carrie was beloved of her husband—never forgotten.

"Well now," Ben said. "Well now." He looked down at the headstone with some pride. "That does look nice, I must say." He took the soaked wrapping off the flowers with some difficulty and shoved it into his coat pocket. He looked around, took an empty stone vase from a nearby grave, and stuck his lilies and carnations into it. "Half full of rainwater already," he said, with satisfaction. "That should do it." He bent down, placed the vase of flowers beneath Carrie's headstone, and straightened up slowly. He took his cap off and stood looking down at the grave.

On the other side of the narrow gravel path was a wooden bench (In Memory of Sybil, Who Rested Here Often and Now Rests Eternally), and Bella tucked her jacket under her and sat down on the wet seat. The skin of Ben's almost hairless head was very smooth and white from the back of his neck to half way down his forehead, and looked distressingly naked and vulnerable to the cold rain falling upon it. She was relieved when he put his cap on again, pulling it down exactly to the shoreline where white skin met brown. Joe jumped up on the bench and sat alertly beside her, watching Ben. She stroked the little dog's head.

"Cancer," Ben said.

"That's how she died?" Bella asked.

"Eight years younger than me. She always assumed she'd be the one left alone. 'Don't you fret, girl,' I used to tell her. 'When I go, I'm taking you right along with me.' She'd laugh at that, Carrie would." He smiled down at her headstone.

"It's so unfair," Bella said, awkwardly, unsure how to offer comfort. If he was grieving, it wasn't in a way she had ever experienced grief. She thought how mysterious the feelings of the old were, as if normal emotional reaction became somehow furred with age.

"Live your life expecting things to be fair and you'll die disappointed," Ben said, coming over and sitting down on the other side of Joe. "Things is the way they are, and that's that."

Bella looked at him, perplexed, and he turned his head to her. His eyes were very blue and there were no tears mingling with the rain on his skin. "Don't believe me, do you?" he said.

Bella pulled back the pink hood of her jacket so she could hear him more clearly. "You don't mind she's dead?" she blurted out before she could stop herself.

"You *are* wet behind the ears, aren't you?" Ben said kindly.

Joe stood up on the bench and shook himself violently, flinging water indiscriminately over Ben and Bella. Then he sat down again with a yawn, leaning into Bella as if for protection against the weather. She put her arm around him, glad of his warm body.

"You dratted dog," Ben said. "Now look what you've done. You just tell the nice lady you're sorry, you hear me?"

"It's okay," Bella said, holding out her other arm and shaking her pink sleeve. "It's gore-tex. The wet just slides off."

"More than mine does," grumbled Ben, pulling his collar up higher. "Catch my death, I will."

"I was just thinking if it was Jonathan," Bella said, trying to find a way to apologize for what she'd said. "My husband. And it was his grave." She shivered.

"You don't look old enough," Ben said.

"I think about him dying a lot," Bella said. "And I always see myself curled up in a little ball. I don't think I'd ever walk or talk again if he died."

There was a silence, both of them looking over at Carrie's grave, the white lilies and carnations brave in the fading afternoon light.

"No point making a fuss," Ben said at last. "Don't do no good. Don't bring her back."

"No, but how do you cope with missing her?" Bella asked. "With her not being there?" Ben didn't answer straight away, and for a panicked moment Bella wondered if she'd said something else stupid—blundered into talking about a relationship that wasn't like hers and Jonathan's, wasn't close in a way she understood and needed. She had never talked with anyone like Ben before. "I'm sorry," she said. "I didn't mean to pry."

"I talk to her," Ben said. "I talk to her and I hear her talk to me. That's how."

Bella stole a glance at him. He was looking at the grave, still smiling faintly.

"That's where she's buried," he said, with a nod. "It's a nice grave, that is. Shows respect." It was his turn to struggle to explain himself to this funny little girl who had a husband and a big house, yet who seemed to have no notion at all about how to get on. But she'd found Carrie's grave for him and Joe liked her, so he tried. "I'm glad to see the headstone and bring flowers and that," he went on. "But that's not where she is really." He paused to catch his thoughts.

"She is buried here, though?" Bella asked, uncertainly.

"She's *buried* here, yes," Ben said. "But she stays with me, like she's always done. She's in the house with Joe and me. Not—" He stopped, exasperated by the impossibility of words.

"Not literally, in person," Bella said suddenly. "But in—in soul."

Ben looked at her in surprise. "Yes," he said. "I weren't sure how to put it. But that'll do. Yes."

"But it doesn't stop you missing her," Bella said.

"Course not." Ben said. "Carrie and me, we was—well, we was close, that's all."

Bella felt tears heavy in her own eyes.

"But I can still talk to her, see?" he went on. "She couldn't take me with her any more than I could of taken her if I'd gone first. That were just to make Carrie laugh. But she couldn't leave me neither. It's hard to lose a person you been with for fifty years."

"I'm sure it is," Bella said softly.

"No, I meant you *can't* lose them," Ben said. "Not really. They're always with you, see? So you take what you got and you go on." He stopped. "Carrie could of explained. I'm no good with words."

"I wish I could have met her," Bella said.

Joe slid down her jacket, laid his head on her thigh, and closed his eyes.

"Cheeky monkey," Ben said.

Bella stroked the dog below his ears, and he sighed extravagantly. "I wish I had a little dog like Joe," she said.

"You got kids?" Ben asked.

She shook her head. "I'm not sure if I want them," she said. "Right now, I just want Jonathan. I don't like to think of sharing him."

"Carrie couldn't have kids," Ben said. "She was good about it, but she minded. We both minded." He coughed, surprised at the admission slipping out.

Bella thought about Jonathan behind his closed door, intent on his work, with the music playing and her depression shut firmly outside. "I don't think Jonathan cares," she said.

"Mind if I give you a piece of advice?" Ben said.

"What?" asked Bella, bending forward so that Ben shouldn't see her tears.

Ben looked at her curled like a child over the little dog. "Time you went home," he said. "You're wet through, you are."

"No, I'm not," she said, sitting up and hunting in her pocket for a handkerchief. "I'm fine."

"Don't tell me," Ben said. "It's gore-tex and the wet runs right off." He handed her a large cotton handkerchief, un-ironed but clean and carefully folded. "But your jeans is soaked and them little red shoe things. You'll catch cold if you ain't careful and then where'll you be?"

"They're rubber," Bella said, wiping her face. "Or rubberized or something. They're quite waterproof." She stuck a foot out. "Just because they're red doesn't mean they're not practical."

"Pardon me, I'm sure," Ben said, accepting back his wet handkerchief and wiping his face with it in turn.

"What were you going to say?" Bella asked, with the clumsy directness that had kept going the longest conversation Ben had had in a year.

"Going to say?"

"'Mind if I give you a piece of advice?' you said."

"Oh that," Ben said. There was a pause, but Bella kept silent, so he was forced to continue. "That husband of yours."

"Jonathan," she said.

"Him." Ben pushed the handkerchief back down into his pocket. "Leaves you to get along by yourself, does he?"

"How did you know?" asked Bella.

"Carrie used to complain about that sometimes. When I was out doing things on my own, like. But that don't mean," Ben said quietly, "that he don't care about you. Don't mean that at all."

"How do you *know*?" Bella fretted.

"You're moping, that's what you're doing. Wandering round a graveyard in the rain and cold when you could be tucked up in that nice warm house of yours. What's he doing, anyway?"

"He's working," Bella said. "He's always working, even on a Sunday afternoon when I made his favourite cheese soufflé for lunch. In his fucking studio, fiddling on the computer. He's a photographer," she added dismissively.

"'Ere, wash your mouth out, young lady," Ben said.

"Sorry."

Ben stood up, grimacing with stiffness. "Time I was off," he said. "Come on, Joe. We got to go look for a bus."

Vanessa Furse Jackson

"Oh, don't go," Bella cried. "Why did you ask what he was doing?"

"Being married," Ben said, taking a jaunty red lead out of an inner pocket, "don't mean trying to be one person." He clipped the lead onto Joe's collar. "Carrie'd tell you the same. She was good about that, Carrie was." Joe sat up, shook himself with a jingle, and reluctantly jumped down off the bench.

Bella watched him, her thigh suddenly cold where the little dog had removed his warmth. "What do you *mean*?" she asked.

"Come along, then, Joe," said Ben. He crossed back over the gravel path to stand by the flowers and the headstone, Joe obediently at his heel.

Ben took his cap off again for a moment, and Bella kept quiet.

"I'll be back in a year, then, girl," she heard him say, as he put the cap back on.

"Ben," she said forlornly.

He smiled over at her. "Put your hood up," he said.

She did as he said, then got up and went to stand beside him, looking down at the raw lettering. *Beloved Wife*.

Ben slipped the red lead over his wrist and put his hands in his raincoat pockets, hunching his shoulders against the fine, continuing rain. They stood in silence for a moment. "You got to care for him, not just care that he cares for you," he said at last. "Ain't that right, Joe?"

"So it wasn't always easy for you either," Bella said.

"Well, of course it weren't," he said. "What do you think? Life ain't given you to be easy."

"What'll I do?" she said.

"Look up there," Ben said, nodding towards the window from which the wet curtains still fluttered like trapped ghosts.

Jonathan stood there with his hands on the sill, a dim figure in the waning light, looking over at her and Ben. His body was strained outward as if to see them better, and his hair was wet from the rain.

Bella turned to Ben. "I'll walk with you to the gate," she said, almost as if the graveyard were her property now, and Ben a welcome visitor she was reluctant to let go.

"We're honoured," said Ben. "Aren't we, Joe?"

The Clinic

Madeleine sat in the waiting room, staring at a recipe for meat loaf in the magazine she was holding. Her fingers were stiff, her bare arms cold and goose-pimply.

"Inoculation against rubella? Yes," her mother said. "High blood pressure? No. Treatment for mental disorders? Really, the questions these people ask." She gestured with her pen at the form the receptionist had handed her then held the clipboard at arm's length, as if she feared contagion.

The close-up of a meat loaf slice with a section of hard-boiled egg in the middle made Madeleine feel hungry and nauseous at the same time. Nervously, she moved the spurt of warm saliva around her teeth. Her mother had tried to make her eat breakfast, but she'd refused the diversion, just as she'd later refused the suggestion of a sweatshirt. She wasn't a *child*. She turned over the page. The magazine felt greasy against her hands.

"Heart attack, mammogram (ridiculous at your age!), stroke. Does any one in your family . . .? I don't know how they expect us to know all this."

Madeleine focused her gaze on a headline: "Why Your Preschooler Suffers from Bad Dreams."

"I wouldn't dream of asking your father if any of his unappetizing relations suffered from high blood pressure or hemorrhoids."

Your father. Daddy. The biological father Madeleine saw once a month for Saturday lunch before he hurried off for an afternoon doing something unavoidable connected with his work. Golf? she wondered. Horse racing? Poker? "One day, we'll spend some real time together, sweetheart," he'd say. "One day when I'm not so busy, I promise."

"Any previous surgeries? No. Pregnancies?"

Madeleine felt her mother's eyes on her. "Many children are afraid of death," the article on preschoolers began.

"You could enter into this a little more," her mother said, tapping her pen on the clipboard. "I might as well be here by myself."

The words of the article swam as tears slid over Madeleine's eyes. A small sound escaped her.

"What did you say?" her mother snapped.

"Nothing."

"Let me tell you, young lady. If there was any way of my avoiding being here, you can be sure I would have taken it."

Madeleine looked at the cover of the limp magazine she was holding. It was eighteen months old. She let it slide onto the chair next to her and rubbed her hands on her jeans.

"Palmer?" said a bright voice. A plump nurse had appeared in the waiting room, a file clutched to her chest, and was holding open the doorway to the sanctum beyond.

A tall girl got up awkwardly and sidled her way across the room. She was followed by a boy in a leather jacket, his hair flopping over his eyes.

"They're not going to let him in there, surely?" Madeleine's mother said.

The door to the sanctum closed.

"One more," Madeleine said, looking across the room at a woman with a pasty, exhausted face and dull hair. She seemed awfully old to be here. There were questions she wanted to ask, many questions, but she could never ask them of her mother.

"One more before us?" her mother asked. "Not exactly worried about timekeeping here, are they?"

Madeleine looked at her watch. At this precise time on any other Thursday, she'd be in English. Right now, she'd be settling down next to Shelli and Lissa for one of Mrs. Bunn's interminable rambles through *Romeo and Juliet*. Mrs. Bunn was obsessed by the stupid play. "Any one of you girls could have been Juliet," she'd trill. "Think of it. Fourteen and in love!" The boys would shuffle in their seats and snigger, and Jake, ever the joker, would say in his newly broken voice, ""Cor, Miss, was it legal at fourteen, then?" And Mrs. Bunn would cry, "Have you no romance in your souls, you children of technology?" and the class would be off to its usual rowdy start, under whose confusion Shelli could begin the texting that would keep the three of them occupied until the bell went.

Her mother had made her leave her mobile at home. Madeleine kept fingering the empty phone pocket of the leopard print bag Lissa had given her for her fourteenth birthday. She wondered if Jake would notice she wasn't there today. She had sent messages to Shelli and Lissa. "ILL 2DAY. CU L8R." But not to Jake.

"There, I think that's it," her mother said. "What a ridiculous rigmarole. I wonder how many more hoops we're going to have to jump through before we get out of here." She got up and took the clipboard over to Reception.

Madeleine watched her walk to the sliding glass window. She could tell by the way her mother stood, ducking her head, that she was nervous, wishing she was elsewhere. Madeleine bit down on her sympathy. Whose fault was it they were here anyway?

This time last year, almost to the day, Jake and she had ridden off on their bicycles for the first time to Petts Wood. There, you could look for sweet chestnuts if you felt energetic, or you could just smoke peacefully, lying on the thin grass between the trees, creating a sanctuary unthreatened by adult mistrust or prejudice. His voice was still that of a boy's then, not so different from Shelli's and Lissa's, and he and she had talked about things that mattered, serious world things, not the everyday gossipy stuff the girls discussed about who was shagging who in *EastEnders* or *Hollyoaks*, or who'd broken up with who at school. Jake had shed his jokey manner, been gentle yet impassioned about what interested him, and for the first time she'd understood how you could have a boy for a friend.

"School is so not what's important," he'd said, lighting her cigarette with an orange Bic lighter.

"So not," she'd agreed, leaning back against the great grey trunk of the beech beneath which they were sitting and sucking in a long drag of smoke. She loved the dizzy wave that surged across the top of her head when she inhaled.

"Hour after hour, we sit there learning nothing whatsoever," he said. "And all because the so-called grown-ups—LOL—dunno what else to do with us."

"They're secretly scared of us is what I think," Madeleine said, looking up through lime-dazzle leaves to the blue sky far beyond.

Vanessa Furse Jackson

"Oh, oh, we've had children, how terrible," moaned Jake in a high voice. "Quick—find somewhere we can lock them up so we can get on with our lives."

"If only they'd let us get on with ours," Madeleine said, flicking ash into last year's beech leaves.

"Think about all the things we could really be learning," Jake said. "When I get home, I go straight to my room and get online, and *then* I start my education for the day. God!" He lay down on his back on the fine hairy grass and shut his eyes.

Madeleine looked over at him, wondering if this meant she could tell Shelli and Lissa she had a boyfriend at last. His eyelashes were much longer than hers.

"Where do you stand on the ethics of stem cell research?" Jake asked, sitting up with a bound and opening the sexily-fringed eyes at her.

"Rackleford," the plump nurse called.

"Rackleford," Madeleine's mother said, not particularly quietly, as she sat down again. "What kind of a name is that?" She began rummaging in her bag.

Madeleine slumped in her seat with embarrassment, as the pasty-faced lady walked across the waiting room and was ushered out of sight.

"At least we're next," her mother said, sweeping her eyes over the people who'd arrived after them. She popped a Tic-Tac mint into her mouth and clicked her bag shut.

Everyone in there looked so miserable, Madeleine thought. All prisoners of the same system. "Can't we just go home?" she whispered.

"We've been through all that," her mother said. "You make your bed— you lie on it. That's what being an adult means."

"I'm *not* an adult," Madeleine wanted to cry out. "I'm a child, and what you're doing to me is wrong." But she said nothing, just turned her head away from the smell of peppermint, imagining the sour breath that lay behind it.

"JAKZ NOT THE 14U," Shelli had texted.

"Y HIM?" Lissa wondered.

Why not? It didn't stop her doing the things with them that they'd always done. Jake was an addition to her life, not some weird kind of interference.

Madeleine shifted on her hard chair. On a table in the corner of the waiting room was a pile of toys—building blocks, plastic cars with big yellow wheels, a couple of cardboard picture books. Was it only on Thursdays that there were no children visible at the clinic? Madeleine imagined the waiting room full of mothers and small children, babies carefully swaddled and rocked in encircling arms while toddlers stumbled around with the plastic cars, unaware of what life would shortly throw at them. "Why Your Preschooler Suffers from Bad Dreams." Because of what their parents do to them, I expect, she thought, with a sideways glance at her mother.

"I've half a mind to complain at the amount of time they think we have to waste," her mother said. "If I ran my business like this, I'd soon have no clients left." She owned a successful hair and nails shop next to the Multiplex—the Multisex, Madeleine's friends called it, disdaining the back row where only the sad and the desperate would think of doing it.

She and Jake had first done it in Petts Wood.

"Airlie?" said the plump nurse, holding open the door.

"At last," said Madeleine's mother.

Madeleine got up half-reluctantly from the hard chair and picked up her leopard print bag. The inner sanctum behind the nurse looked dark, the door a mouth to swallow her up. She followed her mother across the waiting room, shaking her hair down over her eyes.

During the nearly eleven months they'd gone out together, she'd talked more to Jake than she ever had to Shelli and Lissa, who accepted her silences as easily as they accepted her friendship. "You're too deep, that's your problem, Maddie," they said. With Jake, she'd felt more like a shallow stream, babbling away to him as if she couldn't stop, words pouring out of her as he introduced subjects the girls never seemed interested in. War, evil, the corruption of power, Islam, nuclear proliferation. Whether or not to have sex together.

They discussed at great length whether doing it would ruin their friendship, whether abstinence was or wasn't a defiant moral stand, whether waiting until they were surer of each other would make it mean more. In the end, on a hot Saturday afternoon in June, after eight months of deliberation, they pushed their bikes deep into the coniferous section of the woods and simply allowed it to happen, or at least that's what they told each other afterwards. "It felt right." "It was time." "We were ready." What Madeleine had actually felt, lying on a carpet of prickly brown pine needles with the sun filtering down onto her eyelids from a distant, glittering sky, was that if Jake stopped doing what he was doing to her, she'd die. Frenzied, embarrassed by her body's greed, she clutched at him until the act was completed. And it had ruined their friendship. In the end.

Madeleine stood on the wobbly scales, as the plump nurse moved weights back and forth, remembering the feel of Jake's hands slipping inside her bra. She shivered.

"Cold, dear?" the nurse asked. She had little coloured teddy bears printed all over her tunic.

She doesn't approve of me, Madeleine thought. I expect she thinks I'm a whore.

As Jake must have done.

She and her mother sat down where the nurse indicated, on two chairs in front of a desk whose sign read Counselling Services. Madeleine slumped down, folding her bare arms tightly around the leopard-print bag, as if it might offer her warmth.

"Your decision needs to be made quickly," the counsellor said, leaning forward over the desk. "As it is we'll have to perform a D & C. You're almost into your second trimester. You don't want to undergo a D & E, now do you?"

Madeleine hadn't the faintest idea what the woman was talking about. She watched the nurse making notes at another smaller desk. Everything in the room seemed the colour of cream-of-mushroom soup. She swallowed a sudden updraft of nausea.

"The decision has been made," her mother said. "I've signed all the paperwork. I'm not sure what your talking to us is supposed to achieve."

"Legally, Madeleine must receive counselling before the procedure," the woman said. "This is a serious step she's taking." She handed a pamphlet over her desk to Madeleine. "She must be fully aware of what she's agreeing to."

"She's fourteen," Madeleine's mother said. "She's too young for all . . . this." She waved an arm at the desk, the nurse, the counsellor.

Madeleine knew her mother was close to tears. "It's okay," she said, touching her arm.

"It's *not* okay," her mother said to the counsellor. "None of this is okay. She's not old enough to agree to anything."

"Except, apparently, to the act of sexual intercourse," the counsellor said.

"You don't *know* that," Madeleine's mother said. "You don't know she agreed."

"Oh, please," Madeleine said.

"Mrs. Airlie," the counsellor said, patience thick as butter in her voice, "if you cannot remain quiet while I talk to Madeleine, I will have to ask you to wait outside."

Dilation and Curettage, Madeleine read, *involves inserting a spoon-shaped knife (a curette) into the womb to cut the fetus into small enough pieces to suction it out.* She folded the pamphlet in half and then into quarters, clutching it in hands suddenly slick with sweat.

"Have you thought, Madeleine," the counsellor said, smiling at her, "about how you will feel afterwards?"

"Yes," Madeleine said, though in truth she had not. She'd quite successfully switched off all thinking since last weekend when her mother had discovered her only daughter was pregnant and had gone ballistic.

"Do you love the father of this baby?" the counsellor asked, still smiling. Her teeth were very white, Madeleine noticed, and her red mouth was shiny with lip-gloss.

"Don't be idiotic—of course she doesn't," Madeleine's mother said. "How could she understand love at her age?"

Madeleine shrugged and rolled her eyes.

The counsellor nodded to the nurse, who put her notes down and came over to where they sat. "Mrs. Airlie," the counsellor said. "Would you object if I talked to Madeleine alone for a brief while? Just a couple of minutes?"

And something in the way she said this caused Madeleine's mother to stand up and follow the nurse from the room without a word or a backward look at Madeleine.

"She's not really like that," Madeleine said, as the door closed. "She's just upset with me, and you can't blame her really."

Upset hardly described the cold figure that Madeleine had encountered on the landing outside the bathroom early on Sunday morning. "You're pregnant," her mother had said in icy tones that brooked no contradiction.

They had stared at one other, each looking into the pale face that was so like her own. Usually her mother was up and out of the house before Madeleine came downstairs, and her morning sickness had, she thought, passed unnoticed.

"I have smelled it," her mother said. "But I thought I must have been imagining things."

Madeleine looked down, shaky from vomiting, longing to crawl back under the covers again. "No," she said.

"No what?"

"No, you weren't imagining things."

"You *slut!*" her mother said.

And Madeleine, thinking of how many mothers must have said that word to how many daughters, laughed, stopped, hung her head.

"I can't allow it to happen—I suppose you know that," her mother said. "I shall take you to Dr. Crawfurd tomorrow morning and then book you the first appointment I can."

Madeleine didn't ask, "appointment for what?" She knew. She switched off her thoughts. Better to let someone else take charge. Better to remain her mother's child. She felt relieved that someone knew at last.

"Do you love the father of this baby?" the counsellor asked again.

It's none of your business, Madeleine thought. She hung her hair over her face.

The teddy bear nurse came into the room again and took up her notes and her position at the small desk.

"Ninety percent of couples who decide to go through with this procedure split up," the counsellor said, in her gentle, considering voice.

When she'd accepted the fact that there was no other explanation but pregnancy for the missing period, the malaise, the subtle changing of a body she despised but thought she knew intimately, Madeleine hadn't panicked or cried or run for help. She was proud of her reaction. She'd simply said to her inner self, "Okay, so you're pregnant, no big deal. You keep going like you've always done, and in nine months there'll be a baby. You'll cope. Thousands have done it before you. Having a baby is natural." She'd been comforted, impressed even, by her fortitude.

She hadn't told Jake. She'd thought that it would be cheating in some way to tell him, like using the pregnancy just to get him back. Now, though, she wondered if Jake would have liked to know about it—if it would have been fun talking to him about the baby—their baby.

"Do you get depressed from time to time, Madeleine?" the counsellor asked.

Stupid question. Everyone got depressed. Even fucking Juliet got depressed.

"Because this procedure tends to cause depression," the counsellor went on. "It can cause stress, loss of faith, loss of self-esteem, loss of interest in sexual intercourse, anger, anxiety, and even suicidal leanings. Have you thought about any of this?"

"I wish you'd stop calling it a procedure," Madeleine burst out.

"What would you call it?" the counsellor asked.

"An abortion," Madeleine shouted. "An abortion."

They stared at each other for a moment, the word still shuddering in the air.

"Yes, okay," the counsellor said. "Okay."

"I have thought," Madeleine said. "I am thinking." She was thinking furiously. She felt trapped between her mother's angry love and this counsellor's theatrical patience. So reasonable, so all-knowing, so absolutely not anywhere close to where she was coming from. She should have told Shelli and Lissa. They'd have known what to do. And Jake. Jake, of course. *Stupid*, she berated herself. What were you *thinking*?

"And?" the counsellor said.

Madeleine shook the hair out of her eyes. "What happens next?" she demanded, pushing the scrunched-up pamphlet into the middle of the counsellor's desk as she might have pushed a rejected offering of food.

The counsellor looked at the crumpled pamphlet in silence for a moment. Then she said, "You sign this agreement, saying you've received counselling and made your choice based on the guidance given."

"And after that?" Madeleine asked, keeping her voice as flat as she could.

"The procedure . . . "—The counsellor caught herself—"The abortion goes ahead as planned."

"Or unplanned," Madeleine said.

"You have to be sure, don't you see?" the counsellor said with unexpected vehemence, leaning across her desk.

"Give me the agreement," Madeleine said. "I'm ready. Tell my mother whatever you have to."

The teddy bear nurse led her from the counsellor's office down a hallway that smelled of fake pine scent, around a corner, to a row of changing rooms.

Before opening one for Madeleine, she waved her arm at a room opposite and said, "That's where you'll be, if you're interested."

She doesn't like me, Madeleine thought again. She doesn't like Thursdays at the clinic. Trying to pretend she wasn't interested, Madeleine allowed her glance to flick into the room then away again.

"Change out of all your clothes and put on the gown you'll find behind the door," the nurse said. "It fastens at the front. Come out when you're done and wait on this chair here."

Madeleine shut the door of the small changing room. *Do this, do that, sit here, wait there.* She looked at herself in a small mirror on the wall. Her mouth looked set, her eyes dark. She ran her hands through her hair. She sat on the bench beneath the mirror, put her bag down, and kicked off her flip-flops. She put a hand on her belly above her jeans. She looked down at her feet. They looked very small and pink, the toes curled against the chilly tiled floor.

What she'd seen in the room opposite kept inserting itself before her like an obstinate Power Point slide. A long, flat surgical bed covered with clean paper. Two big metal stirrups sticking out of the end, into which, she knew, she'd be required to put her feet, with her legs wide open. She could feel the cold metal cutting into the tender skin of her insteps. Then would come the cold metal of the spoon, the *curette*, on her vagina. She put her hands between her legs and rocked for a moment. Then she picked up her flip-flops and her bag, got up, and opened the door.

The teddy bear nurse was nowhere to be seen. The place hummed with voices, low machines, water running, but it seemed empty of people. Disoriented, she had no idea where she was, but at the far end of the passage was a red neon Exit sign. If it led into the waiting room and her mother, she was sunk. She ran on the balls of her feet, pushed at the door, and slipped through, closing it with care. A stairwell. Concrete stairs. She ran down them, pushed at a door marked Emergency Exit, and was out in the blessed daylight, weaving between parked cars, hopping to put her flip-flops back on as she ran, fumbling in her bag for money for the bus fare home. She ran down the street away from the clinic and turned into the main road, her eyes searching the far distance for a bus. *Please, bus, please come. I have to get home before she does. I have to get home* right now. She ran on down the road, looking behind her until at last she spotted a bus and could race for the next stop, hand outstretched, waving until the sound of the bus's airbrakes told her the driver had seen her.

On the bus, breath heaving, she didn't allow reasoned thought to slow down her pounding heart or lessen the urgency of reaching sanctuary. The time for switching thought on or off was over. She had to act before the sanely managing adult world closed its rational pleas over her head again— before she gave in and *obeyed*.

She ran from the bus stop on the corner of her street down the row of familiar houses to the front door through which her father always refused to come, sitting in his big white Range Rover till she or her mother realized he'd arrived and was waiting outside like a chauffeur.

She scraped her key in the lock, ran past the ringing phone in the hall, up the stairs and into her bedroom, where she shot the deadbolt with a smack before falling onto her bed. Tears streamed down her face, even though something inside her was singing in an elation she sensed she'd feel later. She grabbed her phone from its charger and punched in Jake's number. *Come on, come on.* But there was only the dead computer voice of the answering service asking her to leave a message, and she hung up, sobbing, willing him to take out his phone and see who'd called him.

When she heard the familiar guitar licks of its ring, she fumbled the phone open, dropped it on the bed, picked it up again. "Yes, yes, it's me," she said, too blinded by tears to decipher the caller ID. "Is that you? Is it you?"

"Of course it's me—who else did you expect would be worried sick?" said her mother's voice before Madeleine's fingers could move to punch her off and snap the phone shut. *Shit.*

She sat up on her bed cross-legged, one hand holding her hair from her brow, the other opening up the phone again. She stabbed at the buttons. RU OK? MUST CU 2DAY. MUST SPK 2U URGNT! I LUV U :-)

"Talk to me," she sobbed to the phone. "Text me back. Tell me you love me. Tell me it's going to be okay. Please, Jake, please?"

She waited, her heart thudding.

The small screen stared blankly back at her.

As the seconds passed, so the sobs slowed. She began to feel her room gather its shawl of silence around her. Letting her hair fall over her wet face, she put a hand on the soft, secretive skin of her belly, behind which, invisible in its own created darkness, a baby as small as a walnut was growing. Could it really be true? Rocking on her bed, she shut her eyes and pressed the palm of her hand into the yielding skin.

Inside her, struggling for visibility, there was a *baby*—and more than a baby. There was Jake inside her and Petts Wood and sun filtering down onto her eyelids from a distant, glittering sky. There was the smell of pine needles and a long, sinuous path of possibilities curving away beneath the tall trees. A vast future—another whole world, half frightening—was forming in the deep space of her belly. And in that instant she understood that there was another Madeleine there also, one not yet realized, hardly to be imagined, waiting for her.

"Talk to me," she whispered. "Tell me it's going to be okay."

Sitting quite still now, she heard simultaneously the impatient insertion of her mother's key in the front door and the familiar guitar chords of her phone.

A Nice Day Out

I never saw a man who looked
With such a wistful eye
Upon that little tent of blue
Which prisoners call the sky.

Wilde—The Ballad of Reading Gaol

It was very early when Mr. Whitby awoke. Anxiously, he got out of bed, crossed the room, and with his hand made a face-shaped curve at the side of the heavy curtain drawn across his open window. He was immediately aware of light, velvet red, flooding his pale morning skin, blinding and anointing him with promise. As he retreated into the shadows of his bedroom, it continued to flash as fire behind his eyelids. It was five a.m.

Stumbling a little, Mr. Whitby went into a small white bathroom to shave and have his usual refreshing bath. Sitting bolt upright in the icy water, he loofahed his skin with tingling vigour, singing "Hark! Hark! the Lark" to still his shivering teeth, and thumping his heels gently on the splashy enamelled bottom of the bathtub. *My lady sweet, arise: Arise, arise!* His voice rang melodiously down the overflow drain.

His knapsack was khaki with leather straps, old-fashioned, familiar, much cherished. For over a week, he had been planning what he should take and precisely where each item should be stowed, and when he came into the cheerful green and yellow kitchen, drew back the curtains (nasturtiums rampant), and saw the waiting pile on the table by the knapsack, his heart gave a lurch of joy.

But he didn't hurry.

First he drank a glass of orange juice, then he ate a bowl of Grape Nuts, on which he allowed himself a sprinkling of brown sugar and an indulgent dollop of cream. "Which tastes," he said to himself, scrunching with contentment, "as if it were my birthday." Then he made coffee, enough to fill his breakfast mug and his thermos, and sat at the end of the table, sipping as he watched the red sun lift into gold-flushed air.

As the little carriage clock struck six in the living room next door, Mr. Whitby took his breakfast things over to the sink, washed them, rinsed them under the hot tap, dried them, and put them away where they belonged. Out of the fridge, he took several packages, each one wrapped in waxed paper and inserted into an appropriately sized plastic bag with a label to remind him of what was inside. Into the knapsack went a waterproof cape, a tube of sunscreen (he had delicate skin), a map, a sketchbook and pen, a pocket guide to wildflowers, a slender paperback of Keats' poetry, a first-aid kit, a battered Nikon camera, a pair of binoculars, a bus timetable, a bottle of water, the thermos, an apple, a banana, and the waxed and plastic-skinned packages. Items that he might need to lay immediate hands on, such as the map and the sunscreen, went into the outer pockets; everything else was slotted into its predetermined place inside and the straps tugged tight. Mr. Whitby patted the bulging knapsack with approval. "Clever job, by George!" he said to himself. "Couldn't have done it neater if I'd tried."

He sat down at the table to lace on his walking boots, then he put a pipe, his tobacco pouch, three pipe cleaners, a penknife, a large white handkerchief, a tube of Trebor extra strong mints, and a box of matches into the pockets of his jacket. He wound his watch and strapped it onto his wrist. Finally, patting his inside pocket to make sure his wallet was safe, he stood up and swung the pack onto his back. It should have weighed him down, full as it was, but when he stood up he could imagine he'd attached himself to a helium balloon, so buoyed up did he feel. He took a last look around the green and yellow kitchen, straightened a couple of jars on the formica top, and headed for the hallway, where he picked up a handsome blackthorn thumb-stick from the umbrella stand. His trusty stick, cut years before to precisely the right height, lovingly sandpapered and varnished, indispensable friend. Settling his thumb into its smooth vee, he flung open the front door to the day ahead. Ahh, he breathed. Just the weather for a nice day out.

Indeed, he could not have devised a more perfect morning. The sky had opened out into a pale, clear blue; the sun was still low but a buttery yellow now, with a shimmering golden rim that forecast a fine day to follow. A blackbird was singing in a garden somewhere, the candles on the horse-chestnut over the road glowed with radiant heart, and the air smelled young and fragrant. Mr. Whitby inhaled in giddy delight and set off down the road to the bus station.

As he passed the few other early risers, he perceived envy of his holiday state. The woman in the headscarf, the man in greasy overalls, the two young girls with pale, sleepy faces, all turning as he went by with his cheery "Good morning!", all wishing they were as lucky and free as he. His chest swelled in contentment. *The cuckoo is a pretty bird*, he trilled, *she singeth as she flies*. He strode out in time to his music, his knapsack seeming to carry itself, his thumb-stick bouncing rhythmically on the pavement. At the bus station he bought a paper, but when, at exactly seven o'clock, the bus began to back out of its bay and he was on his way at last, he was too excited to read. He sat hugging the knapsack on his lap and gazing like a truant out of the window.

At first, the bus was quite full—of early workers, he presumed, some in nurses' uniform who got off at the hospital, some with small children to be dropped off at daycare, some briefcased early birds catching worms on mobile phones, a couple of schoolgirls with tennis racquets—but by the time the Mammoth Shopping Mart at the edge of the town had been left behind, he was one of only three remaining passengers. Beyond the new housing development, stark against its sore earth and empty, un-defaced bus shelters, the view from his window began to shed buildings as a man might his cares. The world assumed greenness, dark and thick in the hedgerows by the road, beech-bright across the fields, a hazy sage by the far hills under the sky. The journey took almost an hour and a half and was over in a flash.

As the bus pulled into the village and stopped with a genteel eructation of air-brakes outside the The Wandering Pilgrim public house, Mr. Whitby got to his feet with alacrity and prepared to alight. "Lovely day, lovely," he said to the driver, as he maneuvred his knapsack and thumb-stick around the ticket machine and down the steps. "Going to be a scorcher, mate," the driver said cheerfully.

When the bus had pulled away, Mr. Whitby crossed the road to a bench placed thoughtfully beneath a great parasolled oak. He set his knapsack down beside him on the seat, unbuckled the top flap, and removed the camera,

Vanessa Furse Jackson

which he hung around his neck. He got out the little sketchbook, wrote down the highlights of his journey and made a note of his time of arrival, next to which he drew a little bus with a stick figure standing beside it. He drew an arrow from the figure and wrote The Wandering Pilgrim! at the edge of the page before shutting the book and replacing it in the knapsack. He got out the banana, buckled up the top strap again, and began rummaging in the side pockets. He took out the map and studied it closely, tracing his planned route with his finger and muttering directions to himself under his breath. He took out the sunscreen and applied it liberally to his face, his ears, and the back of his neck. Finally, he strapped up the side pockets and swung the pack onto his back with a little grunt. He stood up, stuck the banana in his top pocket, and took a picture of the pub with his camera. Then he was ready. He looked at his watch. It was almost exactly eight-forty.

Grasping the thumb-stick in his right hand, he breathed deeply for a moment or two, catching a brief echo of the dawn's cool scent behind the stoked air of the morning. Then he turned westward and began walking along the road with long, confident strides, the sun resting warm hands on the back of his head, the day rolling out before him in a gentle downward slope, unsullied and rich with things to come.

"Good morning, good morning," he cried to the milkman, the postman, the woman deadheading roses, the child on the pony. His stick rang joyfully on the road, and his head moved to left and right, left and right, drinking in the perfection of the cottages against the harlequin riot of their gardens.

Come into the garden, Maud, he carolled happily. *I am here at the gate alone.* He was almost out of the village now, and the road was narrowing into an enchanting lane, bordered by thick banks of hedgerows, in which were curds of hawthorn, pink dog-roses and trails of honeysuckle. *And the woodbine spices are wafted abroad, And the musk of the rose is blo-o-own*, sang Mr. Whitby.

As the lane continued its downward unwinding, he took the banana from his top pocket and ate its soft flesh with eager stabbing bites. Cows hung sweet ladies' faces over gates as he passed and blew him bubbling, grassy breaths, and lambs bleated their silly quavering cries from distant hills. Foxgloves and uncurling ferns, cranesbill and stitchwort nodded and leant forward to him from dewy hollows. Pushing the peel carefully into the depths of the hedge, he thought to himself how lucky, how very lucky he was.

Wrens and robins sang to him from the warm leaves as he passed, and the honeysuckle bathed his nostrils in the faint beckoning of long-ago summers when he was a boy unburdened and—he stopped and shook his head for a moment. No burdening thoughts today. He turned and looked back up the lane down which he had walked. He lifted his camera to his eye and snapped a picture. He took out his handkerchief, mopped the back of his neck, and eased the knapsack on his shoulders. Then he walked on, swinging his stick.

At ten o'clock, Mr. Whitby stopped for a rest where a track he was to take branched off from the little green lane. He had come nearly five miles, he estimated, and his feet were beginning to ache. He subsided onto the bank under an overhanging holly, sliding the pack from his back with a sigh of relief and closing his eyes in the dark green shade. Everything blurred around him, and for a moment he wasn't there. There was a wall. There were bars. He opened his eyes wide. Shook his head. "Ah," he said briskly, sitting up straight and rubbing his hands together. "Coffee for the troops! Rations! Fall in line there!"

From his knapsack, he took the thermos and carefully selected a waxed package marked Fruit Cake. He poured coffee into the thermos cup and took a sip, unwrapped his slice of cake and took a bite. "Mmmm," he said, "that's more like it." The coffee tasted even better than it had at breakfast, and the cake, moist and rich, he ate to the last glacé cherry before wiping his hands on his white handkerchief. Refreshed in body and spirit, he reached into the pack for his sketchbook and drew some rather formulaic holly leaves. Beneath them, he drew a stick figure with a recognizable slice of cake in its skeletal hand. This time by the arrow he wrote, The Traveller Rests! and smiled down at the page with pleasure. His momentary lapse in concentration he blotted from his mind. Ten-twenty ack emma, he wrote underneath. Five-mile halt. Condition excellent!

He put away the sketchbook, poured a second cup of coffee, and got his pipe and tobacco out of his pocket. Drawing deeply on the pipe as he lit it in a lazy series of matches, he was almost overcome by the picturesque perfection of the moment—the man sitting at ease on the bank, wreathed in aromatic clouds of finest Virginian, knapsack at his feet, coffee beside him, and ah yes, of course, a book clasped lightly in his hand. Mr. Whitby reached into the pack and pulled out his volume of Keats. A bird was singing cascades of song in the holly tree above him as he opened the book and rather self-consciously began to read. "My heart aches, and a drowsy numbness pains / My sense, as though—" He frowned and skipped on down the page— "the dull brain perplexes and retards—" No, no. He read on, caught and reluctant. "For many a time I have been half in love with easeful Death." He shook his head. No, no, that's not right. "Adieu! The fancy cannot cheat so well / As she is famed to do, deceiving elf." He looked up from the book, confused. The wall was grey, the bars high above him. He shook his head again, squeezed his eyes shut, opened them, and the sun was shining brightly on the green bank across the lane, clusters of red campion (or herb Robert, he wasn't sure) glowing beneath the hedge, the bird singing its immortal song in the holly above him. "Adieu," he said, still upset. "Adieu."

He put the Keats away in his pack and lit his pipe again, pulling at it in irritable jerks until the bowl glowed and crackled and the scene was restored. He exhaled slowly, puffing out his lips in a long whiffle of airy smoke.

Peace returned.

The bird ceased singing, and when the song began again it came from some other tree far across the fields. Mr. Whitby drained his coffee, screwed the cup back on the thermos, tapped the remains of his tobacco onto the ground and trod it underfoot, then inserted a pipe cleaner into the stem of the pipe. No use just sitting around, he said to himself. Stir your stumps there. Shake a leg.

The knapsack seemed to have got heavier since he had eaten and drunk from it, and his shoulders protested as, with an effort, he wriggled his arms into the straps and allowed the weight to settle upon him again. He walked slowly onto the grassy track, aware of faint shooting pains behind his kneecaps. He attempted to loosen his muscles by taking small jogging steps. He felt quite chilled. He turned back to look at his bank beneath the holly tree, imprinting the picture on his mind. He took a photograph and several deep breaths. He extracted the tube of Trebor extra strong from his pocket, popped one in his mouth, and filled his lungs with air so sharply minted it made his eyes water. He straightened his shoulders and headed off along the track. It was ten-thirty-seven.

It wasn't as easy walking on the uneven surface of the track as it had been on the road. There were ruts hidden beneath the grass, sudden holes, and occasionally a large stone. He had to keep a wary eye on the placing of each foot and wasn't able to enjoy the view around him as he had earlier. Jolly yellow and white flowers in the hedge, though, he noted dutifully.

He crunched his mint and began to sing "Pack Up Your Troubles" to elevate his spirits and find a rhythm to march to. One, two, one . . . *in your old kit bag and smile, smile, smile*. Wheezing slightly, he cleared his throat. *What's the use of worrying?* He lurched into the rut again and the pack swung awkwardly, almost knocking him off-balance. *It never was worthwhile*. He stopped for a moment to catch his breath. Must be getting old, he quipped to himself. He looked up and saw that ahead of him the track began to climb up along the side of a hill, not steeply but fairly continuously for a while. Save your breath to cool your porridge, he advised, and walked on in silence, listening to the swishing of his boots through the thick grass while *smile, smile, smile* played an irritating chorus in his head.

His boot slid off into a hidden dip and the pack swung him around again, so that he stumbled and fell onto one knee. "Hell and damnation!", he said, and realized in a moment of pulse-racing shock that he had forgotten his stick. His beloved blackthorn thumb-stick. He had left it leaning on the bank in the dark green shade of the holly tree. He had abandoned his trusted companion. He climbed with difficulty back onto his feet and rubbed his knee. Go back for it? He turned. A high filmy cloud had been pulled like a filtering blind half way across the sky, flattening the light and the horizon behind him to a secretive grey. No, not possible. Forlornly, he took a picture of the track running away from him to indeterminacy. Then he turned again and began plodding up the side of the hill.

Between eleven and twelve-thirty, Mr. Whitby didn't see very much of the country through which he was travelling. He had meant to get out his guide and look up each different flower he passed, sketching rare or beautiful specimens, or perhaps stopping to take photographs. He had meant to search out birds with his binoculars. But he couldn't seem to focus his surroundings as he'd been able to do earlier. He saw only his feet in the clumsy walking boots going down into the grass, down into the grass, down into the grass. Keeping time with his puffy breaths. One and then the next one, his knees aching and the muscles up the back of his neck on fire from the drag of the knapsack.

His day out seemed to have been reduced to a dogged determination merely to reach the destination he had imagined for so long. To keep his back

Vanessa Furse Jackson

turned to the wall in the room he dreaded awakening in.

But then, as he stopped once more to catch his breath, he could suddenly smell it. The tang on the air. The iodine scent of childhood clearing the nasal passages and bracing heavy muscles. He saw that the track had opened out into a wide, close-cropped sward of green, and he understood in a flash where he was. "The sea!" he cried. "The sea!"

He stumbled over the tussocks of grass towards the great void at the end of the track where the cliff fell in slate streamers to the sea below. The air blew its remembered spirit into him, and he was almost running by the time he reached the edge, sobbing for breath, tearing himself out of the knapsack, stretching his arms up high and waving his fists in a triumph of arrival.

The sky was almost totally overcast now, but there was still a thin line of blue straining to hold cloud and sea apart, a bar of brightness over the far horizon. Entranced and exhausted, Mr. Whitby gazed out over the vast skin of water rippled, it seemed to him, by the nerves of the tide beneath it. His own muscles trembled in sympathy. He clasped his hands together. Along to his right, where the cliff plunged down to a little combe, he could see the beach where he had planned to have lunch. The tide was out, the sand a rich yellow, the rock-pools enticingly full and exposed. But alas! He knew that his legs would never carry him down the rocky zig-zag path that he could see as a ragged thread running in and out of the steep grass. Not with the knapsack to throw him off-balance and no friendly thumb-stick to steady him.

He settled instead for a convenient dip near the top of the slope, which gave him some shelter from the wind, and where he could sit with his legs dangling down the grass and his back propped up against the banked earth behind him. As he opened his pack, he comforted himself with the thought that up here he had a magnificent view, magnificent, by George! whereas down on the beach he would have felt quite walled in, claustrophobic even.

Rummaging in the pack, he brought out his array of food packages and studied the labels. There was a hardboiled egg, a cheese and tomato sandwich (whose tomato appeared to have oozed rather), a ham and mustard sandwich, a slice of pork pie, six baby carrots, a twist of salt, two thick slices of cucumber, a small bag of sultanas, a jam sandwich, and five ginger biscuits. There was also his bottle of water and an apple. "A feast, a veritable feast," said Mr. Whitby, rubbing his hands together as he surveyed the spread. He tapped his egg on his head and began to peel it in happy anticipation. Yet he found to his disappointment that he wasn't as hungry as he had thought he would be. He ate the egg and a carrot and half of the soggy cheese and tomato sandwich, but then found himself hesitating. He drank some water. "Must keep up the old strength," he said, and managed a ginger biscuit. But the rest of the food he rather sadly packed up again and dropped back into the knapsack. "Have it later," he muttered. "Have it for tea."

He took out the Keats volume and opened it with some trepidation, although less self-consciously than before. "Season of mists and mellow fruitfulness," he read. Ah, yes, apples, bees, much more promising. The reaper, yes, yes, not grim, very good. "And full-grown lambs loud bleat from hilly bourn; / Hedge crickets sing; and now with treble soft / The redbreast whistles from a garden croft; / And gathering swallows twitter in the skies." Yes, that's autumn all right, he thought. Swallows gathering, winter coming. A fine poem, fine. He riffled the pages of the book. Then shut it.

He rubbed his calf muscles. He shifted his position. He dug the sketchbook out and drew a supine stick figure. Jolly Tired, he wrote by it, and closed the sketchbook. He stared down at the beach below then looked out over the nervous sea. He lay back and closed his eyes.

He dreamed he was lying on a hard narrow bed in a room with grey walls and only one window, high-up and barred. He couldn't get out except through the tunnel in his head. The dream went on and on.

He was awoken by a thud on his eyelid. Then a smack on his cheek. He sat up in distress. It was two o'clock in the afternoon. It was raining.

It was raining! The sketchbook, lying by the open knapsack, had great wet welts on its cover. The camera had slid around his neck to the damp ground and was slippery with rain. His face, his hands were wet. In a panic, he flung everything into the pack and began to strap it up. Then he remembered the waterproof cape, undid the straps again, and plunged a hand down through his belongings to retrieve it. He flung it over his head and pulled its hood up and over his forehead. On his knees by this point, he found he was panting in haste and something horribly akin to fear. It wasn't supposed to be like this. No, no, by George! He tried to breathe deeply. He faced the sea void and opened his eyes as wide as he could against the flung sheets of rain. He kept still for a moment. Amid flashes of red velvet, grey walls, sunlight, blinding rain, he tried to think calmly, rationally. To envision

Vanessa Furse Jackson

the remainder of his day out.

Again, he toyed with the notion of retracing his route in order to retrieve his beloved stick, but in the end he felt it better to stay with his original plan—to curve back inland again on a different series of tracks and paths, until he reached another village where the returning bus would stop. Cut off at least an hour, he murmured sternly to himself. Stout thinking. He got out his map and peered at it, trying to prevent rain falling onto it from his hood and his hands from smearing it. He couldn't locate his own position. Here? No, it must be there with the high cliff and the beach. Yes, probably. So where was his next turnoff? Up there by the hedge running inland, surely. A wood. Then a path, there, yes, that one to the right. Hastily, he folded the map and got up, rubbing painful knees.

He stood in the buffeting rain as he tried to work out how to get his knapsack on while wearing his cape, but the logistics defeated him; if there was a way, he couldn't visualise it. Almost whimpering, he struggled to get the wet cape off over his head. It flapped in the gale and growled and tore itself away from him. He clamped plastic folds of it in his teeth while he fought the damp straps of the knapsack, rucking up his jacket sleeves, scraping hard edges along the muscles of his upper arms. Then he put the struggling cape back over himself again, seeing quite clearly the grotesque shape his humped back must make beneath it. Pulled the hood over his head. Stood with his legs planted wide to find his balance. "Bloody rain, bloody rain," he shouted, and felt momentarily better. He began to plod along the cliff, closing his right eye against the bruising slant of the storm.

He reached the hedge and turned left onto a small track that ran along the far side of it. It was such a change to have the rain at his back instead of slamming into his right side that he opened both eyes again and looked up from his feet. "Whew!" he said, puffing his lips out slackly.

He couldn't see very clearly what lay in front of him. The path and the hedge curled around and down to a wood, but the grass had dimmed and the trees seemed drained of colour in the grey air. Beyond them were either hills or clouds—he couldn't tell which. Only the hedge beside him was still solidly present, leaves dark and wet, red haw things and blackberries glistening and heavy with water.

Best foot forward, came the words, and he tried to think of a song to sing as he blundered on through the sopping grass. *It's raining, it's pouring, the old man's snoring* was all he could think of, but he couldn't remember a tune that would fit. His hands were cold and he put them into his jacket pockets, laying them uncomfortably on top of the muddle of pipe, matches, penknife, tobacco, mints, handkerchief, already there. He tried to whistle, but his lips were too stiff. *And couldn't get up in the morning.*

In the wood, there was respite from the wind, but leaves were swirling down from the trees like a different rain, sticking themselves onto his face, sailing across his line of vision, coming straight for him then flying up and over his shoulder in disconcerting swoops. It was dryer under the trees, except that every so often the wind would burrow between branches and rocket past him like a bully, tipping a fistful of raindrops down on his head as it did so. The plastic hood over his ears amplified sound, so that he leapt with fright every time the water exploded on his head.

He trudged on. Reached the far end of the wood. Found a path to the right. One foot in front of the other, down in the mud, down in the mud.

For an hour or so, he barely looked up. His trousers were wringing wet from the knees down. His feet were icy, his boots squelching and sliding. He could no longer move any part of his face. His neck and back and hips and ankles all hurt. His eyes watered uncontrollably. His nose dripped. Motion slowed. Faltered.

What stopped him in the end was the path itself. Long wires of bramble shackled his legs, tore at his cape, and undid his bootlaces. Roots laid their booby traps for him across the path. Bushes had to be fought around or through. Branches dipped lower and lower, and hedges squeezed closer together on either side of him. He ducked and sidled and dragged and pushed. But he was finally brought to a complete halt, baffled by great serried ranks of brambles that rose before him, implacable and impenetrable.

He looked around him. The rain had stopped, but the light had not returned. Indeed, it seemed in a curious way to be failing. Mr. Whitby felt a moment of panic, which he choked down by retreating a few paces from the massed brambles, taking off his cape, and removing the leaden knapsack from his back. He was too stiff to ease his muscles by stretching, but the relief of dropping his burden on the ground was immense. He stood for several moments bathing numbly in the sensation of weightlessness. "Re-group," he heard as if whispered from a great way off. "Re-group."

He bent down obediently but painfully and fumbled open a side pocket

Vanessa Furse Jackson

of the pack with uncooperative fingers. Not there. He opened a second pocket. Not there either. A third. He undid the main strap and delved into the pack, pitching everything out to get a better look. He scurried his clumsy hands around the empty inside. He tried the side pockets again. He stood up with some effort, spots swimming before his eyes, and scrabbled through his jacket pockets. Pipe, tobacco, penknife, pipe cleaners, matches, mints, handkerchief. No map.

The panic tried knocking at his heart again, but really he was too tired for alarm. Tired and a little dizzy. What did it matter, when all was said and done? He didn't have the faintest idea where he was, so a map wouldn't be of much assistance to him anyway. He was on a path that had ended. He had lost his map and his way. No good crying over spilt milk, eh?

He peered at his watch. It had stopped.

He left the waterproof cape and the empty knapsack and the packages of food and the books and the thermos and all the other heavy and useless props of his nice day out strewn on the ground where they had fallen. He turned around, indeed, without looking at them, and began to shuffle down the path away from the dead end, noting absently but gratefully that someone had been decent enough to flatten the grass and brambles and push useful holes through the undergrowth to help ease his way.

He found another path that seemed less overgrown, the trees barer overhead. He pushed on down that until he reached a gate that led out into a field. The gate was metal, ice cold, and padlocked shut, but Mr. Whitby didn't stop to wonder if he did or didn't have the strength to climb over it. He put his flaccid hands on the top and very slowly pulled himself over until he stood shakily on the other side, his back humped over with effort. It was so dark by now that he couldn't see what lay on the far side of the field, but that no longer seemed to matter. He began to walk out over the bare, ridged earth.

Adieu.

The bent figure of Mr. Whitby grew smaller and smaller as it crossed the fading landscape, until it vanished altogether into the winter night.

Before the Fall

Cassie was tired and, being tired, cross. She stared across the breakfast table at her sister and brother-in-law. "I am not ready to go," she said. "And you're damn well going to have to wait till I am ready. What's wrong with you both?"

Matthew glanced sideways at Gemma, and they involuntarily smiled at each other.

"I thought we were supposed to be on holiday," Cassie went on. "What's the big rush?"

"Sorry, Cassie," Gemma, who was also tired, said. "There's no rush. It's okay, relax."

"Dad," Gavin said, ignoring his mother and his aunt. "What's the highest point along the coast?" He had long since finished eating and had a map spread out on his lap.

"It's quite a good idea to get there before too many other people turn up," Matthew said to Cassie, patiently. "Most holiday-makers are slow to get moving in the morning, so it can be the best time to be out." He turned to his son. "About 150 metres, on our bit of the coast—see if you can find it on the map. We're going to be walking there today."

"I'm holding up your good intentions, you mean," snapped Cassie.

"Embury Beacon, cool," said Gavin.

"I think I'll just go and make a start on packing my things up," said Matthew, removing himself from the breakfast table and going upstairs.

The two sisters listened to the stairs creak, to his footsteps moving overhead.

"God, he's such a good little boy scout," Cassie said.

Gavin looked up at her, disapprovingly.

"What's wrong with you, Cassie?" Gemma asked. "PMS?"

"Sorry, Gem, sorry," Cassie said. "I'm stiff from yesterday, and I didn't sleep well, that's all. I'm out of sorts. I'll be okay."

"Uncomfortable bed?" asked Gemma, sympathetically. Like many rented holiday cottages, theirs was rather basically furnished.

"No, the bed's all right. Bit soggy in the middle but all right. No, it's the damn quiet," Cassie burst out. "How can you stand it?"

"The quiet?"

"At night. The quiet. And the dark. I mean, like total dark. I feel as if I'm breathing in black velvet and slowly being suffocated by it. Death by darkness—horrid."

"You should plug a night light in. I've got a spare one I could lend you, if you like," said Gavin.

"Oh, Cassie, you urban animal," Gemma said. She laughed. "Quiet at night is what it's supposed to be."

"All very well for you to talk," Cassie grumbled. "You live in the country anyway. I'm used to noise at night, streetlights. And I'm not going to be much of a support to you if I can't sleep, am I?"

"Shhh," said Gemma, with a glance up at the ceiling.

"You could borrow my radio, Aunt Cassie," Gavin said.

"Thanks, Gav," said Cassie. "You're a pal. But for God's sake don't call me Aunt—it makes me feel about a hundred and one."

"You're a great support, Cassie. I'm glad you're here." Gemma smiled at her sister.

"Oh, crap, I'd better be a good little holidaymaker, I suppose. I'll go and find some aspirin, then I'll be ready to leave," said Cassie and followed Matthew upstairs.

Gavin folded up his map and began to carry the breakfast things over to the sink. He looked at his mother, still sitting staring into her coffee cup. "What's PMS?" he asked.

"Nothing you want," Gemma said.

Later, sitting beside Gavin in the back seat of the car, Gemma watched with envy as her sister gradually shed her grouchiness and became animated, map-reading them through the lanes, teasing Matthew on his careful negotiation of the myriad blind corners and steep hills, squealing as he narrowly missed a cock pheasant who leapt from a bank in front of them. In Bude, it was Cassie who jumped out of the car and bought their lunch pasties at the Landsdowne Bakery while Matthew parked illegally outside the shop, waiting for her. Cassie and Matthew and Gavin seemed to Gemma to have formed a unit, content in their holiday roles, while she, who should have been at the core, remained outside her family. Gavin couldn't keep still—he spent most of the drive leaning forward over Cassie's shoulder, so he could help her read the map and at the same time ask questions of his father. He was ten and ever-hungry for information. Is that a rook or a crow, Dad? Why are the clouds going that way if the wind's in the south-west? Dad, what's 150 metres in feet? I am grateful that I can sit here peacefully and not be involved, Gemma told herself. I can watch them like a film, and at the end of the film I can simply get up and leave. Right, then.

Today, they were walking north up the coast from Welcombe Mouth to Sandhole Cross. Yesterday, they had done Morwenstow to Welcombe and back, the strenuous walk that had made Cassie so stiff. Their plan was to walk the whole of the North Cornwall and Devon coastal path from Duckpool to Clovelly in a week, a trek that enchanted Gavin, who hadn't been at all sure at first that he wanted to be dragged along on this boringly adult holiday, with not only his mother but also his aunt tagging along. But "Dad, that's so cool," he had said. "How many miles will we walk total?" With only one car, each day's walk consisted of following the coastal path until a judged halfway point had been reached, and then returning via a more inland route, if possible, and next day picking up the coastal path where they had left off. Once, Gemma thought, she, too, might have been enchanted by the plan.

The last half-mile of the drive to Welcombe was down a rough track fraught with potholes, and Gemma and Gavin got out of the car to save it from bottoming out. "Nobody's making me walk an inch farther than I have to today," Cassie said firmly. "I'm riding with Matt."

As Gemma walked, watching the car lurch and jolt along in front of her, she wondered why it was so easy for Cassie to talk to Matthew and so hard for her. What were they laughing about now, the two of them bouncing in the front seats?

"Why does she call him Matt?" Gavin asked, with such eloquent distaste in his voice that, despite herself, Gemma laughed. "Dad *hates* being called Matt."

"Well, perhaps he doesn't mind Cassie doing it," she said.

"She calls me Gav," he said. "Eugh!"

"You like her," Gemma protested.

"Yes, but I wish she wasn't here," he said, unexpectedly.

"Why do you wish that?" Gemma asked.

"You, me, and Dad. That's who it should be," he said, and then ran ahead of her, as if embarrassed by his admission. Just like his father, she thought— can't bear to talk about anything that matters. *I wish I was at home, going about my normal routine, camouflaged by the busy-ness of work, house, school, garden, meals, cleaning. It's too exposed out here.* She looked at the pale pink dog-roses in the hedge beside her, so pretty and frail. She looked over the hedge at the little valley, with its fast-flowing stream running down to a final, unstoppable waterfall onto the beach. She looked over to Knap Head, the great thrust of cliff they were about to climb, and saw two people near the top, tiny and crouched, crawling slowly up the cliff path like insects. *Five hundred feet, had Matthew said? I can't get up there,* she thought. *I haven't the will or the strength.* Her legs felt weak suddenly, as if she hadn't eaten breakfast.

In the small car-park above the beach, they all donned boots and rucksacks, taking, under Matthew's supervision, waterproof jackets, sun hats, plenty of water, two mobiles in case of emergency, the lunch pasties, dried fruit and chocolate for energy, *and lord knows what else,* thought Gemma, tiredly shrugging on her load. *He's so careful, so . . . so all-prepared—yes, a good boy scout.* She looked over at him helping Cassie to get her rucksack adjusted, pulling a strap tighter, frowning in concentration. He hadn't helped her. She felt pity for herself as a weight on her shoulders, a stone dragging down her rucksack.

Gavin hadn't waited for the grown-ups to finish their interminable setting-off fuss. He had gone ahead to the stream, had found the stepping-stones across, and was squatting on the far bank when the others caught up with him. "Look, Dad," he said. "There are little fishes in here. What do you suppose keeps them from getting swept downstream and over the waterfall?"

"Goodness, what a boy you are for asking questions," Cassie said.

"If they did fall over, Dad, and they could swim down the beach, could they survive in salt water?" Gavin said.

"It would depend on what kind of fish they were," Matthew said. He always tried to answer Gavin's questions. "Salmon, for instance, travel from seas to rivers. But do you think your little fish would survive their fall?"

"Be great if you were sitting on the beach and salmon started raining down on your head," Cassie said.

"They'd only rain down on your head if you were sitting right beneath the waterfall," said the practical Gavin. "In which case you'd be sitting in the stream."

"Which would be pretty silly of me, wouldn't it?" said Cassie, cheerfully. "Come on, Mr. Literal-Head. Let's get moving."

Cassie was the imaginative one when we were children, thought Gemma. I was always looking for facts and answers like Gavin. She sees pictures, forms connections that make the world look more interesting. I wish I could do that. Unbidden, there came an unwelcome leap of thought. Matthew and I haven't said anything to each other at all today. Not one word. She felt short of breath suddenly. How many days are there when we don't speak to each other?

The others had started walking towards the cliff. Matthew turned and stopped for a moment. Gemma began to walk forward as if he had called to her, and he turned around again and went on, following Cassie's pink T-shirt and purple rucksack up the path. Pink and purple, thought Gemma. Typical Cassie.

The path up around Knap Head was expertly made—a series of steps cut and then held on their vertical sides by boards to prevent erosion. As it zig-zagged its way upward, it revealed to the climbers first the sea and the beach beneath them and then the little inland combe running away back into the hills, green and secret. Both views were extraordinarily beautiful, and Gemma felt the stone lifting a little from her back as she began the ascent. The sun was dodging in and out of small white clouds, the sea was sparkling and flickered with gold, and the cliff was a glory of flower colour—yellow, pink, red, purple, white, green. I can just about do heather and gorse and foxgloves, but I shall have to ask Gavin what all the others are, she thought.

"Don't look down," she heard Matthew say from above her. "Look only at where you're going, at the steps."

Gemma rounded a corner and there he was, with his arm around Cassie's shoulders.

Vanessa Furse Jackson

"She went dizzy on me," he said to Gemma.

"Cassie?" said Gemma.

"I'm okay, don't worry," Cassie said. "I just looked down for a second too long, that's all." She was leaning with one hand on the cliff face and the other clutching one of Matthew's rucksack straps. She looked pale, fragile in the bright sun.

"Do you want to go back down?" Gemma asked her.

"No, no. Down's worse than up. I'm fine, really." She let go of Matthew, turned with great care, and began to climb upward again, conscientiously looking at her feet.

"She doesn't suffer from vertigo normally, does she?" Matthew asked Gemma.

"She's doesn't really like heights," Gemma said, with a sudden vivid memory of a twelve-year-old Cassie's terror at having to climb down a copper beech tree that she had dared Gemma to climb up with her. In the end, Gemma had had to go for help, and their father had come with a ladder. "But it's never stopped her doing anything that I can think of. She was fine yesterday."

"I'll keep an eye on her," Matthew said and set off after her.

Gemma followed slowly, wondering. She had phoned Cassie in a panic ten days before the holiday to beg her to join them. "I can't face all that time alone with him, having to be all holiday happy," she had said, in tears.

"What's the *matter*?" Cassie had asked. "And anyway, I thought Gavin was going, too."

"He is, he is, but I just can't face it, Cassie. I need you, I need you to be my support. Please?"

"Is he being a bastard?"

"No, no, it's me. I can't explain. I can't talk to him," Gemma had said, still crying, and Cassie had agreed to come. But did she hate the idea of walking the cliff path? Gemma asked herself now.

She toiled on up the path, her legs leaden and her breath getting shorter and shorter. Now, she, too, was looking only at her feet, forcing one to pick up, and then the other. Why do we agree to do these things? she castigated herself. This will just go on and on until I die, up, up, up. She didn't raise her eyes until she almost fell over Cassie's outstretched feet. "Sorry, didn't see you," she gasped and sat down beside her.

Cassie was sitting on the grass, with her back propped against a stile, drinking from a water bottle. Her colour was back, and she looked cheerful again. Gavin was sitting on one step of the stile and Matthew on the other. "You haven't half taken a long time, Mum," Gavin said.

"Leave her alone," Matthew said. "She's doing just fine."

"For an old lady, you're meant to add," said Cassie.

"Speak for yourself," Matthew said. "Gemma is young and beautiful and needs no help from either of you."

Gemma swung around in surprise and looked up at him. He smiled and so did she. "I'm doing all right," she said, and thought tentatively, is that true?

"So far," said Gavin, ignoring the adult exchange, as he usually did, "I've seen two ravens, six rabbits, and a buzzard." He had a notebook out on his knee, and was making lists.

"What flowers do you have?" Gemma asked him.

"Foxgloves, heather, gorse," he said.

"Yes, I know those," she said. "What are all the little ones?"

"Just hang on a minute," he said. "I was getting to those. Sea campion, birdsfoot trefoil, kidney vetch, clover, thrift. Which is also known as sea pink," he added, shutting his notebook with a satisfied flourish.

"How does he do it?" said Cassie, admiringly. "I get as far as daisies and buttercups, and that's it."

"Oh, Cassie, you urban animal," said Gavin, in exactly the same tone as his mother had used at breakfast, and they all laughed.

Is this how the others feel all the time? Gemma wondered. Light and free? Am I imagining the dark? Imagining that Matthew and I are no longer close, connected? "Oh, I wish I *was* wrong!" she exclaimed suddenly, and Cassie put a comforting arm around her and said, "You are, idiot child, you just don't see it," as if she knew quite well what Gemma was talking about, and that was more comforting still.

"Come on, you lot," Matthew said. "We may have done the worst bit, but it's still uphill all the way to Embury Beacon and lunch." He climbed over the stile, nudging Gavin off the other side, and they set off together up the next incline.

Cassie and Gemma got up slowly and stretched. Cassie put her water bottle away, and they both clambered stiffly over the stile. "My God, I'm

Vanessa Furse Jackson

going to be fit by the end of this holiday," Cassie said.

"Do you really have vertigo?" Gemma asked.

"Only if I look down," Cassie said lightly.

"You should never have agreed to come with us," Gemma said. "I wouldn't have asked you if I'd known."

"Yes, you would," Cassie said. "You needed me. And I don't mind being needed, okay?"

"I'm not really that selfish," Gemma said.

"When you're depressed, it's impossible to see beyond yourself," Cassie said. "That's why you need someone to do it for you. And Matt doesn't know how to do that yet. Hence me."

"You think he could?"

"He's a good man, Matt. You don't know how lucky you are," Cassie said.

"Hands off," Gemma said.

Cassie turned round and looked at her sister. "The hands have never been on," she said. "Trust me. Trust Matt."

"I don't think he loves me any more," Gemma said. There, it was out, the splinter, wicked and sharp.

"Do you still love him?" Cassie asked.

Gemma drew in a breath. "He doesn't talk to me any more," she said. "He never asks me what's wrong. He doesn't care," and as she walked along in the fragrant sunshine, she wept.

Cassie stopped and caught her sister's arm. "Look," she said. "Stop crying. Look."

Gemma wiped her eyes, tried to stop the flow.

"Look around you. It's beautiful here, the green below and blue above, and even I can tell that there's a skylark singing somewhere near—you'll never get closer to Eden than this place. Up in front of you are your husband and your gorgeous son." Cassie was flushed and earnest, her tone intense. "You have a good job, an adequate income, a little house in the country, your health, and you're making yourself miserable. Wait till you have a real tragedy in your life before you start the wailing and gnashing of teeth. You are innocent of grief, mourning without cause for sorrow. Why, Gem?"

"I'm afraid," Gemma confessed.

"Matt is not going to leave you. It's never occurred to him," Cassie said.

"I know—it's not quite that." How to explain the nameless fears, the anxiety, the desire for Matthew to be somehow different, more attuned.

"You dissect everything too much, Gem," Cassie said. "You're always looking for answers to things, always wanting to know what isn't knowable in the way you want it to be."

"I don't want certainties," Gemma said.

"You'll probe your marriage to death, if you're not careful," Cassie said. "And yourself along with it. Just be here, Gem. Here." She swept an expansive arm before her. "You own all this beauty. It's yours for the taking, don't you see?"

Gemma tried to smile. "It's Matthew I want," she said.

"Do you know what he said to me in the car when you two were walking this morning?" Cassie said. "'Aren't I lucky?' Just like that. 'Aren't I lucky?' We both started laughing, it was so out of the blue."

"He said that?"

"He meant because of you two," Cassie said.

"You don't know that," Gemma said.

"Oh Gemma!" Cassie said, exasperated, and began walking again.

After a moment, Gemma followed her, and they didn't speak again, but she felt better than she had, as if something tight within her had loosened, at least for the moment. She looked around her. The grass on which they were walking was springy underfoot, and, over the fence to their right, sheep were calling in their plaintive voices. There *was* a lark singing, and from the left, beyond where the grass suddenly stopped in mid-air, came the distant boom of the sea below. The path they were following did indeed continue to ascend, but it was a gentle ascent compared to the scramble up the cliff steps, and Gemma realized with a shock that she was glad to be here.

"Cassie," she yelled to her sister, hastening to catch her up. "Sorry!"

Embury Beacon, the highest point of today's walk, had been chosen as the lunch spot by Matthew, who liked a good view and knew that everyone preferred going downhill after they'd eaten. When Cassie and Gemma reached it, he and Gavin were standing waiting for them.

"Look at it. Look, Mum," Gavin said in a rush.

"Look at what?"

"This is Embury Beacon. Isn't it brilliant?"

Gemma looked. A wide semicircle of rough grass, a sensation of being above everything around them, the coast spilling away from them in a curve to the north-west, leaving a sweet glimpse of the sea. "It's lovely," she said. "A good spot to be alive in."

Matthew smiled. "Yes," he said.

"Yes, but don't you see?" Gavin said, impatiently. "Look at the banks around it. It's an old hill fort, isn't it?"

They looked. "Is it?" Cassie asked. "How do you know?"

"I read about it in a book at the cottage," Gavin said. "Those are its ramparts. Do you think if we started digging, we'd find anything, Dad?"

"I'm quite sure it wouldn't be legal," Matthew said. "But I'll tell you one thing. Berry or Bury is Anglo Saxon for hill, and it became the English word barrow or burial mound. I'll bet this is a mound. It's old all right."

"Oh, wow," said Gavin. "Dad, supposing I just dug down a rabbit hole— that would be okay, wouldn't it?"

"Lunch," said Matthew firmly. "I'm starving, even if you aren't."

"Good diversionary tactics, Scout Master," said Cassie, and laughed as Matthew cuffed her. They all straggled over to the far side of the circle where the view was spectacular and sat down with some relief.

The pasties were a bit squashed but still warm, and they tasted ambrosial in the tangy sunshine. "I hope my choices were all right," Cassie said. "I got lamb and mint for Gem and pork and apple for me, but I didn't think the men would take to anything but straight Cornish."

"Mmmm," said Gavin, through a mouthful of flaky pastry.

"Lamb and mint. Whatever next?" said Matthew.

Gavin drank coke and the rest of them drank cider, which Matthew had carried up there in a cooler in his rucksack. There were apple and cherry tarts to finish with, and Gemma lay back in the grass and groaned. "I shall die," she said. "That was wonderful. Worth every minute of the climb." She heard Cassie laugh, and thought to herself, I should hold on to this moment forever. The sun was warm on her eyelids.

"Come on, Gavin," Cassie said. "Let's go and explore before the cider hits my legs."

"How can it hit your legs?" Gavin said, and Gemma heard their voices fading as they moved off and she moved closer towards sleep.

"You'll get a pink nose," Matthew said.

Before the Fall

Reluctantly, Gemma rolled over onto her front. "Ouch," she said. "There are prickles in the grass." She pulled the nearest rucksack over towards her (purple—it was Cassie's) and laid her arms and head on it.

"And maybe snakes," added Matthew.

"Really?" She lifted her head.

"I'm teasing," he said.

Looking at the blurry purple beneath her arms, Gemma said, "Do you like Cassie?"

"Do I like her?"

"Yes."

"Well, of course I do," Matthew said. "She's your sister."

There was a short pause.

"She does talk a lot, though," he added.

Gemma kept quiet, closed her eyes.

"It's what I like about us," he went on. "We don't need to talk all the time. Peaceful."

Gemma smiled into the rucksack, drifted.

She wasn't aware of having slept, but when she raised her head the sun hurt her eyes, and in the harsh dazzle she wasn't sure where she was.

"What happened?" It was Matthew, and his voice was flat with shock. She half turned.

Matthew was kneeling in front of Gavin, gripping him by the arms. Gemma thought urgently, I am still sleeping. This is a dream.

"Where?" Matthew was saying. "Where, Gavin?"

And Gavin said, stuttering, "There were s-some sheep that had got stuck on a ledge. We leaned over to look. She just f-fell."

No.

"Which way, Gavin? Where were you?"

"She didn't make any noise, Dad. She just fell."

No.

"Where?"

"She just fell," he repeated. "She's lying on the beach."

Gemma let out a sound and sat up.

"Stay with Mum," said Matthew. He got out his mobile from a pocket in his rucksack and stood up. But when he began to run back along the path, Gavin was glued to his side, one hand clutching his father's sleeve.

Vanessa Furse Jackson

"Cassie," Gemma whispered. She looked at the lovely sparkling landscape, at the two figures getting smaller. Above her, she could hear a lark singing its spiralling song. Her heart raced, her mouth was dry, skin clammy. "Please, God," she heard herself saying. "Let me wake up." She shut her eyes against the golden sunshine and saw instead an incongruous spot of pink lying gaudy on the grey rocks five hundred feet below. "When I open my eyes," she went on stubbornly, "they will be here, and it will be downhill all the way to Sandhole Cross and the lane that will take us back to Welcombe."

The Albert Memorial

From the little house in Braintree Street, it was an easy walk to Bethnal Green tube station. "Fortunously," as Victoria had so often remarked to her husband. "Otherwise, I doubt you'd peel yourself off that couch and go anywhere."

Albert would sigh, aware that silence was golden but unable to resist going for the silver. "I am not yet, contrary to your expectations, unable to rise to any occasion," he would say, with a quiet dignity that left his wife unmoved.

"You wouldn't rise to your feet if you didn't know you could sit down again in two shakes of a duck's tail," she'd say, and Albert would turn over a page of the *Daily Mirror* with as much care as if it had been a tissue leaf of the bible.

"You'd trample up any excuse to stay lolling around all day like royalty." And Victoria's delighted wheeze of laughter would squeeze a smile out of Albert behind the sheltering paper. She was a card, she was.

From Bethnal Green, you could take the Central Line all the way to Lancaster Gate, which couldn't be more convenient if it tried ("now could it, Albert?"), and when you came up from the underground, there were the twin parks, the verdant empire of Victoria's dreams. "And it belongs to you and me just as much as it belongs to *them*," she would say, when she saw the big green space glinting through the rush of traffic along the Bayswater Road. In through the Marlborough Gate to the fountains of the Italian Gardens, and it was like choosing between a sapphire and a ruby, as she would remark, happily. Turn left for Hyde Park and the Serpentine—turn right for Kensington Gardens and the Round Pond. And, of course, Kensington

Palace, from which augustus building, a royal might so easily alight. On a red carpet day. As she said this, Victoria would heave a reverential sigh for the ghost of Princess Diana.

Victoria found it difficult to articulate precisely why she was so drawn to the parks. If asked by acquaintances, she would say magisterially, "They're London's finest lung," a phrase she had read in her guide book, but to Albert she said, "It's that equality and fraternizing, isn't it?", which, although she'd also read the words somewhere, came closer to her own feelings. "Don't matter if it's the rich man or the poor man at his gate, we all breathe the same air here," she told him. "Good, fresh, pricey air, given to the people of London in perpetualness. Why waste it?"

Sometimes Victoria came on her own, but mostly she managed to lure Albert off the couch by a combination of dire threat and picnic. "I've made paste sandwiches," she'd say. "You like those. And Marmite and strawberry jam. And bananas. And if you don't come and help me carry the basket, it'll be tinned pilchards for supper. Without toast."

Helping to carry the basket meant carrying the basket. It was an immense, soft basket you could have carried a baby in, and Albert loathed having its floppy bulge wedged under his arm for the afternoon. He felt people must be looking at him, wondering what kind of a dippy joke he was. But staying home alone, while delightful for the first hour or so, became an increasingly uneasy affair as the clock ticked nearer to the point of Victoria's return. He was, in fact, unable to remain peacefully on the couch with his favorite coronation mug full of tea (or something stronger). To appease the impending wrath, he'd begin some ingratiating job, from which he'd pace to the front window and back a million times before he rushed down the little hallway to open the front door to his wife. At that moment, the wrath, unappeased, would fall onto his hapless head anyway. It wasn't worth it. He sometimes called her Your Majesty to himself, but to her face she was Victoria, or, on mellow occasions, Vick, old girl.

He actually quite enjoyed the picnics, sitting on a bench by some water or close to the Peter Pan statue, where he could watch the children fingering the little gnomes and fairies in the Elfin Tree while Victoria made offhand remarks about people who never grew up. He enjoyed the lavishness of the sandwiches, unheard of for tea in Braintree Street, and the brilliant beds of flowers that he didn't have to weed or water, and she was right, the old girl, though he wouldn't tell her so—there was a kind of bond, a head-nodding good will, between the people there. It was like being at the seaside, Albert thought, all of us away from our old familiar places and indulging in a nice little outing together. It made him feel quite playful sometimes. "Almost as if we're courting," he said to her on one occasion, leaning towards her on the bench and waggling his banana.

"Not that you'd know how to court a one-legged lepercorn in a thunderstorm," she said.

He'd been quite hurt. "I knew once," he said. "I won you, didn't I?"

"Faint words never won no fair lady," Victoria said, sipping tea primly from her plastic thermos cup. "I decided you could skip the courting and go right to the 'eart of the matter, if you remember."

He did remember, blimey, yes. "Love's young dream," he said soulfully.

"Love, my foot," Victoria retorted. "Don't be such a soppy bugger." She smiled at him suddenly, her eyes as blue as a girl's.

Picnics were all right when Vick was in a good mood.

No, it was all that physical exercise he disliked, the endless paths, beg pardon, *walks*, she made him follow her down, the heat in summer, wet shoes in winter. That effing Moses basket. If only he could just sit down and stay sitting down. Albert was the king of observers, at his most content when he was watching others scurrying, quarrelling, jogging, pottering, galloping, hollering, living energetic lives that were not his. He loved watching sport on the telly, not because he was a fan of any particular game or team, but because he revelled in watching all the silly arses running about while he lay pleasantly supine on the couch.

In Hyde Park, he liked nothing better than watching the riders in Rotten Row. "Route du roi, actually," Victoria had told him, something to do with an old monarch, according to her guidebook, although when Albert cast his mind back to Kings and Queens of England and his history teacher Miss Clutterbuck's massive bosom, he couldn't recall any Roys. He liked Rotten Row anyhow, whatever it was called. He particularly enjoyed the lady riders in their jackets and helmets, a shuttle of wide pale bottoms going up and down, up and down from the rude haunches of their horses, and them thinking they looked so posh an' all.

Not such good entertainment in Kensington Gardens, although he liked watching the theatre of little kids lined up by the Round Pond, mouths

Vanessa Furse Jackson

agape at the remote-controlled boats of the bigger kids, destroyers that raced around sinking the listing yachts. He could remember when all the nannies wore uniforms. A few did even now, but mostly you couldn't tell the difference between the nannies, the mums, and the older sisters—all of them with the gawky legs and gaudy flair of flamingoes, gossiping in flocks away from the naval maneuvres.

As long as no one asked him to join in, get involved, take sides, make decisions, Albert was a happy man. He would have been happier still, he thought, if only Her Maj didn't demand quite so many royal duties of him. He'd once tried suggesting a divide and rule policy. "I live my life, you live yours. What's wrong with that?" he asked, knowing, even as he spoke, that he should never have opened his mouth.

"Live and let live?" she'd scorned, as he closed his eyes. "Live and let die more like. You'd wither away like a raisin on the vine if I wasn't there to sustenance you, as you know very well."

He heard her soft wheeze of laughter at her own riposte.

"We're married, in case you'd forgotten, Albert. Bound together in sickness and in 'elf."

Bondage, Albert thought, gloomily.

But it wasn't a bondage he chafed at very often—just down the pub when a ritual wife-despising session accompanied the pints and darts. He couldn't imagine life without Victoria.

Sometimes, they would traverse the empire almost to the road that bordered its southern reaches, which was called successively Kensington Road, Kensington Gore, Kensington Road, and Knightsbridge, to Albert's consternation. "Gore?" he would say, shaking his head. "Gore? What kind of bloody name is that?"

Victoria never got Albert's jokes.

Usually, though, they would stop earlier and find a bench by the Serpentine, Peter Pan, the Pond, sometimes the Bandstand or, on one of Victoria's vigorous days, the statue of Physical Energy down Lancaster Walk. "Look at that, will you," Victoria would say, rummaging in the crèche and setting the thermos of tea on the bench between them. Albert, slumped on the seat, his aching legs stretched out before him, would obediently look, but the statue did nothing to revitalize his flagging body. Or spirits, he thought, though come to think of it spirits sounded just what he needed.

"What a body," Victoria would exclaim, handing him a plastic mug of strong, lukewarm tea. "You can 'elp yourself to a sandwich. I'm not your servant."

"More sugar?" Albert would plead, able to mouth her response by heart.

"No amount of sugar would make you any sweeter, Albert, so just you lay off, you hear me?"

"I'll just have to get my strength back with a jam sandwich, then," he'd say in a weak voice.

"Can't see 'im eating sugar, now can you?"

Albert regarded the splendid physique of the statue with a disfavour fed by the unfairness of the competition.

"George Frederick Watts," she said. "Bronze."

She knew a lot, he had to admit that. Her and her guide books. She ought to charge people to take them round the parks, not waste her time with him. He'd look at Physical Energy again, at the huge horse and rider, trying to imagine the grossly muscled, naked figure on that big old charger trotting sedately down Rotten Row. Blimey, that'd hurt, wouldn't it? But he'd like to see the lady riders' faces.

From the Watts statue, they could see, right at the end of the broad, tree-arched walk, the Albert Memorial and beyond it, clear only on sunny days in leafless winter, the domed lid of the Royal Albert Hall across the road from the park. But they rarely went that far and, if they did, never stopped to look at the Memorial. For a start, it was all boxed in with scaffolding for ages. Falling apart, they said. Albert was sorry in a way. He'd have liked to examine his namesake, sitting up there in the top tier of that bloody great wedding cake. But even when the scaffolding came down, Victoria wasn't keen. "You don't want to go 'aving your 'ead turned by all those Albert thisses and Albert thats," she said, looking down the walk one cold bright day at the newly distinct monument. But they both knew Albert wasn't one to have his head turned. It was Victoria's reluctance that kept them away. "Gives me the willies, that thing does," she said with a shiver. "Can't say it convicts me one little bit that she loved him."

"Course she loved him," Albert said, nodding at the monument. "Plain as the nose on your face."

"Catch me putting shrines up all over the place when you're dead. You'll

Vanessa Furse Jackson

have a little urn on the mantelpiece and that'll be your lot."

Albert was dying to ask her what made her think he would be the first to go, but wisely he held his counsel. He knew better than to encourage loitering so far from Lancaster Gate and the warm smelly tube ride home.

But Victoria's willies came back to haunt her the following winter. For Albert did die first, following a chill caught after a bleak east wind and tossing rain had suddenly caught them unexpectedly by Peter Pan. One day a cold, the next pneumonia, and he was snuffed out, just like that, as she said over and over at the little gathering in Braintree Street after his cremation. Dust to dust and ashes to ashes, just like that. Till Death us apart, and then just like that, he's gone. You wouldn't believe it, would you? Just like that. She couldn't touch the sandwiches she'd made.

She didn't go back to her green empire for some time after his death, which had shaken her to the core. Worthless, good-for-nothing, work-shy, bone-idle retrograde that he'd been, she felt as if she'd lost her balance when he'd gone, as if she might fall down in the street without him there beside her. She put the urn on the mantelpiece and next to it a photo of him in his stiff black suit at her nephew's wedding. It did not bring comfort. The house was empty of his presence, unutterably silent.

She stayed in Braintree Street for the rest of the winter, going out only to her part-time job at Mr. Patel's minimarket, shopping there and nowhere else. Albert would have encouraged her to go the parks, she knew, but without him there to leave behind, she couldn't bring herself to make the effort.

It wasn't until early May, on a morning when the sun seemed to have travelled all the way east from Lancaster Gate especially to shine in her bedroom window that she got up the courage to go. Into a canvas shoulder-bag, she put her guide book and a banana, and set out for Bethnal Green station. Albert had given her the bag for Christmas, just a month before he died. It had the London Underground logo and Mind the Gap inscribed on it, and he'd been hurt when she wasn't amused by his choice. She didn't ask herself why she was going, didn't worry and fret her mind around the thought, as Albert would have done, but just went. She felt a bit wobbly to begin with, but she knew it was time.

The hardest moment was coming out of the tube at Lancaster Gate and making herself cross the Bayswater Road. When she reached Marlborough

Gate, she checked. "Your empire," he'd called it, and for once she hadn't corrected him. Today, though, she didn't feel the confidence of ownership. With no Albert by her side, she felt out of place all of a sudden, hesitant to enter the familiar space.

"Get on in there, Vick, old girl," he said.

She started. "Albert?" A woman whose poodle had stopped to do its business on the first available blade of grass inside the park looked around and stared at her.

"It belongs to you just as much as it does to her," Albert said. "Remember?"

"Well, I never," Victoria said gratefully, choosing the path that would avoid Peter Pan but lead her towards Lancaster Walk.

The day was soft and blue, the grass emerald, the trees a darker, uncurling green, bending inward to each other like guards of honour high above her head. When she reached Physical Energy, she stopped and sat down on a bench to eat her banana, eyeing the distant Albert Memorial with a degree of nervousness.

"Don't worry," he said. "No harm in looking." And then, as she still hesitated, "All part of your empire, isn't it?"

"I always found it ghoulyish," she said. "All that money and how many sculptors to build it?"

"Dozens, probably," he said, cheerfully. "But what's it to you?"

"Over a dozen, anyhow," she said. "And some of them died before it was finished. Died on the job, as you might say." She looked down the walk at the familiar shape. "I mean, you couldn't go there and sit quietly and think, like you can to a grave. Or a urn," she added, as a pair of joggers, bumping into each other as they turned to look at her, thumped past the bench.

"Why couldn't you, then?" Albert asked.

"Well, you'd have been in your carriage," she said, frowning as she imagined the scene, "and all the populars following. It stands to reason there'd be no privacy."

"P'raps the thought of it just being there was a comfort to the old queen," Albert suggested.

"She wasn't old when he died. Only forty-two, poor little creature." Victoria sighed mournfully.

"Good thing I hung around longer than that then, wasn't it, Vicky?"

Vanessa Furse Jackson

"They spent ten million pounds on restoring it, did you know that?" she said. "And don't you Vicky me."

"Must of known you was coming, then," he said, and she thought she heard him laugh.

"Ten million," she repeated. "It doesn't seem right spending all that money on a piece of dead sculpture."

"Excuses, excuses," said Albert.

"Oh, all *right* then," she said. "I'll go and look at it, but on your own 'ead be it." She dropped her banana skin into a bin, picked up the Mind the Gap bag and started off down Lancaster Walk towards the Memorial. "Putting up a great monster like that to your husband," she muttered as she went. "Whatever next?"

A grinning policeman in shirtsleeves halted beside her. "You all right, Gran?" he asked.

"Bloody cheek," she said, without pausing to give him the time of day.

"Quite right, too," said Albert. "None of 'is bleedin' business."

They reached the end of the walk together.

"It's not that much of a thing, anyway," she said, hovering at the back of the Memorial with her empire behind her. She was of half a mind to turn and begin her journey home.

"Just a peek, eh?" Albert coaxed.

So she went round the edge of it, and there she was stopped. She stood looking down the wide sweep of stone steps, across Kensington Gore to the round red curves of the Royal Albert Hall, and then back up at the bronze gilded figure beneath its soaring steeple. She felt a wave of awe wash through her, which she resented bitterly. "This isn't for me," she said. "All this pomp and circumstances. I don't want this."

"Give it a chance, Vick," pleaded Albert.

"When did I ever listen to you?" she said, but she stayed where she was and even took her guidebook out of the bag. "I'll probably get pigeon mess on my coat," she said, crossly, "and then you'll be in trouble."

One of the great sculptural achievements of the Victorian era, she read. One of the priciest, too, I wouldn't wonder, she thought. *Notice the groups depicting the Continents and the Arts and Sciences.* Groups of what, may one ask? *The magnificent frieze has over a hundred and fifty carved figures, angels and virtues.* Carved virtues? She looked up in a vague obedience, but her heart wasn't in it.

"I thought it'd make you feel better," Albert said, sadly.

"Well, it doesn't," she snapped. Then, as he'd been considerate enough to accompany her here, she tried to explain, fumbling on with thoughts that seemed all of a tangle. "It's as if," she said, "I'd put up a shrine to memorize you, and round the shrine I'd put angels and things I'd read about. Virtues," she added scornfully.

"Instead of?" he asked.

She thought hard. "A real shrine," she said, "would have your couch in it." She heard him laugh softly. "I know it sounds daft," she said.

"I did court you once," he said. "And I bloody well won you."

"Maybe," she said. "And a Daily Mirror and your coronation mug and the TV remote. Oh, I'd find other things, but you get my point. They'd be *your* things." She put the book away and turned, a bit stiff from standing. "All right," she said. "I'll walk round Your Highness's throne once, then it's off to find the tube. I can't be malingering here all day."

A little herd of people with bright T-shirts and cameras, who'd been staring up at her from some lower steps, broke up and jostled away as she began to move. "They think I'm talking to myself," she said, and managed a small laugh of her own for the first time that day.

She walked slowly around to the front of the Memorial. It certainly was clean, she'd give it that. Almost as good as new. And it was nice to see all that scaffolding gone. She craned her neck and looked up at the gleaming giant, seated with one foot higher than the other, one arm carelessly on his knee, the other holding something that looked like a stone book—probably the Bible or a book of Continents or something, she thought. Not the Daily Mirror, that's for sure.

She brought her eyes down from the dazzle of the figure against the blue sky, and there, below all the gilded fuss, was carved the one word, ALBERT.

Not Prince Albert or Prince Cohort or Prince of whatever foreign place he'd come from. None of that Latin and Greek so ordinary people couldn't read it. Just ALBERT.

Victoria's heart raced.

"See," Albert said, "she did love him, then."

"Yes," she said, putting a hand to her chest for a moment. "Albert," she

Vanessa Furse Jackson

said. She stared till the word blurred, then lowered her eyes and walked on around the Memorial and back up to Lancaster Walk.

Albert didn't follow her across the park, but sitting on the swaying, noisy tube, she pictured him waiting for her to get home to Braintree Street. Had the poor little queen pictured her Albert, too, coming in and out of the rooms of all those palaces for the forty-odd years after he'd died? Had he talked to her? She'd heard his voice clearly enough. She could see him now, lolling back on the couch, watching the football with a mug of tea in his hand. When he heard her key in the lock, he'd come with a sliding rush of feet down the little hallway to open the front door for her.

Grieving for Man

He died of black lung. It took thirty years, for he was a lean, strong man when he first went down the mine, but in the end it took him, as it had taken his brother and two of his uncles before him. Miner's asthma, silicosis, coal workers' pneumoconiosis—it didn't matter what the doctors called it. He coughed up black muck from scarred lungs, he hunched over in his chair trying to catch his breath, and his lips and fingernails turned blue as lavender flowers. When even the oxygen tanks the National Health provided failed to relieve the pain of gasping, gasping for hours at a time, the ambulance came and took him away to hospital for a stay in the lung ward. And one time he was there, a time that had seemed no different from all the other times, he died.

For Mary Batsford, it was the end of years spent keeping the husband she loved alive for just a little longer. "Don't go yet," she'd implored him through so many congested winters. "I'm not ready. Not yet." And she'd hand him his new inhaler from the doctor before going to the kitchen to brew another hot jug of Friar's Balsam, whose pungent steam, breathed in beneath a tented towel, she privately thought a good deal more efficacious than any doctor's prescription. She'd sit by his chair and read the newspaper to him when he was too tired to hold it. She'd buy the Famous Grouse Whisky she couldn't afford because it made him smile and call her his lovely girl in the evenings. She'd scour the *Radio Times* to find shows he'd enjoy on TV—football matches, ballroom dancing, drama series set in the rugged North of his childhood, *Coronation Street*, sheepdog trials. And she'd let the children from next door come in to see him on his better days, a little hurt at how much he looked forward to their company, rationing them to the thirty minutes it took before he'd begin to fight for breath.

For the children, his death marked the end of that portion of their lives in which nothing bad ever happened. They would never again place blind trust in parents who said soothingly after a frightening dream, "We're not going to die. No one you love is going to die. Go back to sleep, now— everything's all right." Man was dead, and nothing was all right.

"They shouldn't call you Man," Mary used to say to him. "You should ask them to call you Mr. Batsford." *Or Tom*, she might have added, except that she was the only person left who called him Tom now, and in her mind flitted a superstitious dread of sharing his name with anyone else.

"Man," he'd say in his whispery voice. "If that's what they see me as, who 'm I to say otherwise?"

"But Tom," she'd protest.

"Stripped bare. An essence. Man," he'd said, and that was that.

And then he was gone.

When their mother broke the news of his death to Sara and Patrick, the children stared at her, wide-eyed and still, their identical messenger bags full of homework trailing from their hands onto the kitchen floor. "They tried everything at the hospital, I gather," said their mother, who believed in telling her children the absolute truth at all times. "They put something called an endotracheal tube down his throat into his lungs and hooked him up to a machine that would breathe for him, but it was no use. His heart failed, and he died at 4.30 this morning."

"Why didn't you tell us?" Sara asked, her face white.

"Before we went to school?" Patrick added. Fifteen months apart in ages, they still finished each other's sentences as twins might.

"Mrs. Batsford came round here when she got home from the hospital," their mother said. "You'd caught the bus by then."

"You should've told us," Sara insisted.

"The moment you knew," Patrick said. "Man was our friend."

"Poor old thing," said their mother. "She was in an awful state. I must remember to take her round some food tonight, or I'm sure she won't eat. I don't know how she'll go on with him gone."

"Poor old thing!" Sara exclaimed. "What about us?"

"He was our friend," Patrick repeated, and the two of them, staring at their mother, broke into sobs they couldn't control, filled with disbelief that she couldn't take this first dreadful grief from them.

When he'd become too ill to work any longer, Mary had brought Tom down to the mild air of the South, to her mother's small terraced house in Newbury, far from the coal dust and smoke-filled pubs and working men whose hollow, lined faces foretold their early deaths. If he missed these familiar associations, Tom never complained. When her mother died, the little house became hers, and she settled down to her task of making Tom well again. She planted hydrangeas and sweet Williams and hollyhocks in the tiny space at the front of the house, and in the long thin garden at the back she made herb beds and vegetable beds and a fruit cage for her strawberries, raspberries, blackcurrants and gooseberries. She baked bread from whole-wheat flour, made soup from her vegetables, bought chickens and sausages from a farm shop at the end of the bus route, and made salads from the lettuces and herbs in her garden. She bought Tom a velour armchair for the living room, against whose high back he could rest his head, and she bought him a canvas reclining chair so he could sit out in the garden on sunny days. She bought him vitamins and homeopathic remedies from the health food shop. She cleaned the little house with a fierce energy to ensure that no dust, no blanket fluff, no mites, no germs, no harm should come near him. She watched him like a mother dog with one weak puppy, snapping at anyone who came too close, curling herself around him as she waited for his breaths to grow quiet and strong.

Sara and Patrick were the only people apart from the doctor whom she allowed into the house, and this concession was granted only because they slipped beneath her guard one day when she was in the town buying Tom a new fleece jacket at Marks and Spencer's. He suffered badly from the cold. The children were seven and not quite six then, and Tom was smitten by their healthy, guileless grace.

"Hello, Man," Sara had said, standing in the doorway of the living room, hand-in-hand with her smaller brother.

"Who is Man?" Patrick had asked.

"He is," Sara said. She ventured farther into the room, looking around her as she did so. "I'm Sara. He's Patrick."

"We haven't seen you before," Patrick said politely, coming to stand before Tom's chair. He was a fair sturdy child, whose blue eyes looked with friendly openness into Tom's.

Vanessa Furse Jackson

Tom smiled at him.

"We live in the house next door," Sara said, twirling a piece of her ash blonde hair with one finger. "We moved."

"From London," Patrick added.

"Pleased to meet you," Tom said.

"Our father works in London," Sara said.

"He goes on a train every day," Patrick said, with envy in his voice.

"Does he now?" Tom said, amused at the information they thought to bestow on him.

"But Mum says London isn't safe any more," said Sara, with no trace of concern.

"So we moved next to you," Patrick said, putting his hand on Tom's knee.

"Well, isn't that nice, then?" Tom said.

"Except we don't have any friends here," Sara said.

Tom looked at Patrick's hand on his knee. "You'd be welcome"—he took another breath—"to come again."

Sara gave him a wide, gappy smile. "We'd like that," she said, standing on tiptoe to touch a yellow china bird on the mantelpiece.

"What's this?" Tom said, taking a coin from his pocket.

Sara turned. "Fifty pence," she breathed. "For us?"

"What's half fifty?"

The children looked at each other. "Twenty-five," they said together.

"Twenty-five each," Tom said. "Of course. Come again. Be glad to see you."

"Good to have children about the place," he'd said, silencing Mary's protests with his unspoken reference to the children that had never been born to them. He'd touched her hand. "You don't mind, do you, my lovely girl?"

She had minded at first, but she'd grown used to their appearances in the three years since then, even learned to look forward to their visits. The house seemed brighter when they were there, charged by their zest and impatient curiosity. Sometimes, before they went to talk to Tom, they helped her weed the garden or pick peas or raspberries for his supper. Sometimes she'd bake a cake for them, which Patrick would write on in squiggly icing, and Sara liked watching her knead bread on the kitchen table. But what they really came for was to stand one either side of Tom's chair, in the small cave of the living room or out on the sheltered patch of grass by the back door when it was warm enough, and have conversations with him. They'd pick a polite bowl of fruit or vegetables, watch her for a while in the kitchen, then one of them would say, "It's time to talk to Man now," and they'd be gone from her side to his.

They talked and he listened mostly, nonsense talk, she'd often think, as she worked in a different part of the house or in the garden nearby, where she could keep half an ear cocked. Once or twice, she overheard him telling them about his old life in the mine, which upset her, although she wouldn't say so to him. She didn't want him harkening back to those times he'd left behind—she wanted him to be happy here, to look forward to the future, their future. She'd listen to the children's chatter then wait for the low rasp of his voice, chiding herself at the relief she felt each time he offered this proof that he still lived. When thirty minutes had passed, she'd shoo the children home and sit by him until his breathing settled again.

When she got back from the hospital where he'd died, she sat down in her usual chair in the living room, clasping in her hands the plastic bag of his pajamas and fleece jacket and slippers that they'd thrust into her arms as she stumbled away from his body. She looked across the gas fireplace at the high-backed armchair that bore Tom's imprint in its old velour flesh as clearly as if his spirit still sat there. The perpetual sound of his breathing had been as insistent and as absorbed into her being as the tick of her father's old clock on the sideboard. Without it, the house seemed to have had the life sucked out of it, to have been reduced to no more than bricks and plaster, doors, window frames, bones. She sat without moving until the clock chimed the hour, then, rising with a sudden urgency, she placed the plastic bag on his chair and hurried out to tell someone, anyone, that he was dead, as if the telling might make it not so.

"I know he's dead," Sara said, "but I can't believe he's dead, if you know what I mean."

"Yes," said Patrick, who usually did know what she meant.

Kneeling on her bed in the back bedroom they shared, Sara looked out of the window at the neat brown garden next door, "all put away for winter," as Man had said. "One day, they'll be putting me away for winter," he'd added and laughed his wheezy, infectious laugh.

"He talked to us only last weekend," she said. "He wasn't dead then. He had those tubes in his nose, but he wasn't dead at all."

"How could he have gone to hospital without us knowing?" Patrick asked. His head ached from crying, and there was a curious heaviness inside him, as if he had eaten a round grey river-stone for his supper.

"They never think to tell us anything," Sara said, giving her pillow a thwack. "We're just the children, remember?"

"Man would have told us," Patrick said.

"Yes, he would," Sara said, and the tears spilled hot and splashy over her hands as she tried to wipe them away.

"Don't cry, Sary. Please don't." Patrick's voice wavered.

"We should at least have been allowed to say goodbye," she said, blowing her nose on her sheet and scrubbing the tears away angrily. "Couldn't they even think of that?"

"Could we . . ."—Patrick hesitated—"Could we write him down somewhere? So we don't forget? Put him in our computer?"

"We'll never forget him," Sara said.

"Yes, but . . ."

She turned away from the brown garden and looked at Patrick, small and hunched on his bed. "Yes," she said. "Yes, okay. Good idea. But not in our computer. They could look in there. In a book."

"A book," Patrick echoed.

"Tomorrow. Tomorrow I'll find us a secret notebook, and we'll write down everything we can remember he said to us."

They spat into their palms and shook hands.

In the night, Patrick vomited, and their mother, looking at Sara's heavy eyes in the morning, kept them both from school. "Pat needs to stay in bed, and it's Friday anyway," she said, pouring cornflakes into a bowl and handing it to Sara. "Your father won't mind. I'll tell the school it's something you ate. But you must go round and visit poor Mrs. Batsford. Tell her how sorry you are and so on. She's been very good to you children."

"But I can't," Sara said in horror. "What would I say? I can't."

"Just something to comfort her," her mother said, leaning across the table to pour milk over the cornflakes. "You knew Mr. Batsford quite well. He was good to you. It's only right you should go."

Sara stared at her mother. Mrs. Batsford was a grown-up. She, Sara, was a child. Children didn't go and offer comfort to grown-ups. It was supposed to be the other way around. What was her mother thinking?

"Eat your breakfast," her mother said, "or the cornflakes will go soggy."

In the little house next door, Mary sat in her chair in the wintry morning light, watching the imprint in the velour. She, who had thought for both of them for so many years, was waiting for Tom to tell her what to do next. The undertakers chosen by the hospital had phoned. "Yes," she'd said. "Yes, yes. Thank you." She couldn't remember what they'd asked. Sara and Patrick's mother had brought round a ready-made fish pie from Sainsbury's the evening before, which still lay in its package on the kitchen table where she'd put it when the woman left. *Taste the Difference*, it said on its label. She wondered if she ought to throw it away, but there didn't seem much point as Tom wasn't here to share it with her.

She'd folded the pajamas and placed them on the arm of his chair, hung the fleece jacket over the back, and put the slippers down on the two depressions in the carpet where his feet had rested each day. There didn't seem to be anything else to do. The house, which she'd loved less because she'd grown up in it than because it had contained Tom's hard-won breaths for so long, had been rendered inanimate, its dust, she supposed, no longer an enemy. So what would Tom tell her to do?

"Hello," said a tentative voice from the doorway.

She turned her head. It was Sara. For a moment, their glances locked across the gloom of the living room, each seeing the other as an insubstantial figure made ghostly by the nebulous grey light. Then Sara's eyes slid to the empty chair and flickered away again. She'd grown tall, Mary saw, her hair still very fair and scrunched back in one of those untidy pony-tails that young girls wore these days. It made her look older than her ten years, yet something distressed in her eyes brought Mary to her feet. She must find words to comfort the child. "Thank you," she said, "for coming." She felt dizzy, standing up suddenly like that.

"Man is dead," Sara said in a small voice.

"Yes," whispered Mary.

"How could he just die like that?" Sara asked. "Just . . . go?"

"Oh, my dear," Mary said, and went over to put her arms around the child.

As she felt Sara's warm body within her embrace, and as Sara's hands reached around behind her to rest lightly on her shoulder blades, Mary felt the calm membrane that had sealed her in its cling-film all morning irresistibly dissolving. The girl was now the same height as she was, the same height as Tom had been ("Two peas in a pod, we are," he used to say when they stood or lay entwined), and it was, in that moment, as if she held some vital incarnation of him, strong and whole again. Surrendering to it, she laid her head on Sara's shoulder and wept in shuddering sobs more wracking than any she had suffered in the thirty years of his dying.

Sara, aghast, held on to the shaking shoulder blades, her own body rigid with inadequacy and revulsion. A grown-up. Crying. Like a mad person. And no one to help. She wanted to cry herself. She stared hard at the china bird on the mantelpiece, a sour, alien smell in her nostrils, yearning to run from the claustrophobic, empty little house. She held on in silence until the sobbing quieted, then, unnerved, she dropped her arms.

"What am I going to do?" Mary said in a hoarse voice. "What am I going to do without him, Sara?"

Sara looked at the streaming nose, the reddened eyes, encircled with puffy, wrinkled skin, and looked away again in repugnance. This was not anyone she knew. Not anyone she should have to know.

"I'm sorry, Sara," Mary said, hunting in her pocket for a handkerchief. "I didn't mean to . . ."

"Sorry, Mrs. Batsford," Sara said in a rush. "I came to tell you. That he's dead, I mean. Patrick's sorry, too, only he was sick in the night and couldn't come."

Mary tried to smile at her, a handkerchief raised to her trembling lips, and Sara turned and fled.

"It was awful," she said, crouched in a shocked rage on the end of Patrick's bed. "Awful, awful, awful." She was out of breath from racing up the stairs, panting.

"It sounds scary," he said, looking interested despite the dark shadows beneath his eyes.

Sara knew her reaction made her a bad person, knew how upset her mother would be to hear her talk like this about poor dear bereaved Mrs. Batsford. "But it's what I feel," she burst out. "That dreadful old woman bawling on my shoulder. You've no idea. I could smell her breath. Ugh." Overwrought, she put her head in her hands and wept.

Patrick crawled down the bed and put an arm clumsily around her. "Don't cry, Sary," he said. "You won't have to go again, I promise."

"I'm crying for him," Sara said, comforted. "Not for her. Mrs. Batty."

"I found a notebook while you were gone," Patrick said. "And I wrote *Mans Book* on the cover, look. I thought we could start by putting in about the canary."

"Yes," Sara said, sniffing hard. "Yes, okay." She felt shaky inside. "Let's think about him, not her. Give me the book."

"And you can use my new liquid gel pen," said Patrick, handing it to her with the notebook.

"Tell me what to write first," she said.

"How they walked. Write how they walked."

"We had to walk between the rail lines," Man had told them.

"You had a railway down in the mines?" Patrick had asked, entranced.

"Underground railway. That's right," Man said, winking at Sara. "We had to walk on the sleepers. Between the lines. Till we got to where we were working, see?"

The two children were standing in the living room, one on each side of him, their hands on the rug over his knees.

"Go on," Sara said, envisioning him walking on the sleeping bodies of exhausted miners. She never quite knew whether to believe his stories or not.

"Hard to see in the dark, beyond our lamps. And us carrying enough powder bags to break our backs," Man said. He had to stop every four words or so to suck in his whistling breaths, which only added suspense to his tales.

"What happened if you didn't walk on the sleepers?" Sara asked.

"Did you fall?" said Patrick.

"Often at first," Man said. "But you learned."

"You learned what?" Sara said.

"To keep your eyes on the canary up front," Man said.

"A canary?" Sara said. "A real little bird, d'you mean? Alive?"

"In the mine?" breathed Patrick.

"Firedamp was the problem," Man said. "Gas that collects near the roof or floor of the mine. If it's not mixed with enough oxygen, it can kill you. The silent enemy, we called it." He stopped and lay back in his chair, wheezing.

Vanessa Furse Jackson

"Go on," Sara said.

"About the canary," Patrick said.

"Man in front carries a canary in a cage," Man said, his head still back. "We all watch to see if the little chap's still alive. Breathing. The moment he falls off his perch, we scarper."

"You leave him there in the deadly gas?" Sara's voice was anguished.

"It goes in his lungs and he dies?" Patrick added, his eyes round.

Man looked at their stricken faces. "A lot worse things happened than canaries dying down the mines," he said.

"Poor little bird," whispered Sara.

Man relented. "They used to take canaries down the mines, it's true," he said. "But not in my day. They had better ways of detecting the gas by the time I was working." He watched the children begin to relax. "You great pair of softies."

"Oh, I'm so glad," Sara said, gripping his knee and surreptitiously wiping her eyes.

"But we did have several canaries in an aviary on the surface," Man said. "Safety Department looked after them. Kind of mascots, you might say. The lads were that fond of them."

"But not down in the dark?" Patrick said, wanting to be sure.

"No, it was just the men they put down in the dark," Man said gravely.

"I'm so glad," Sara said again.

"Hand me the little china bird off the mantelpiece, would you, Sara?" Man said.

"The yellow one?" Sara said, putting it into his hands. She drew in a quick breath of realization. "Oh. It's a canary."

"That's right. Belonged to my brother. His mascot, if you like." Man stroked the little bird's smooth back.

"I didn't know you had a brother," Sara said.

"You didn't tell us," Patrick added.

"It didn't save him in the end," Man said, still stroking. "Died of . . . well, never mind. We've all got to go some time."

"But you have his canary," Sara said, encouragement glowing in her voice. "So now it's your mascot. And you're still alive. That's what matters." She leaned forward and touched the bird's head with her finger.

"That's what matters, yes," Man said. His breath whistled. "Life and being decent to one another. Good thing to remember."

"Decent?" Patrick asked.

"Kind," Man said. "Being decent, being kind. Makes the world go round. Believed that till he died, my brother did."

"Time you were running on home," said Mrs. Batsford from the doorway.

"She always used to come in just when he was about to tell us something extra specially interesting," said Patrick, watching his sister's pen move enviably fast across the pages of the notebook.

"She didn't like him having fun with us," Sara said. "I think he liked being with us more than with her, if you want to know the truth."

"Poor old Mrs. Batty," Patrick said.

Mary didn't see much point digging, raking, or sowing seeds in the brown garden after Tom was gone. She watched from the window as groundsel and ground elder and a few straggly nettles came up into the spring air. If she didn't put her glasses on, the green fuzz of weeds looked almost as if everything out there was normal—as if she'd planted after all, and later would harvest young carrots and runner beans and purple sprouting broccoli for Tom's supper. The gooseberries ripened golden in their cage and fell to the ground unpicked. She went out one day and took the netting off, so the birds could strip the bushes. When she bumped into her neighbour at the little Spar Grocers on the corner, she offered the strawberries to the children, if they'd come over and pick them. "How very kind," said the children's mother, but Sara and Patrick never came.

Eventually, Mary was able to put away the pajamas and fleece jacket and slippers in the chest-of-drawers in the bedroom. She folded up the tartan rug Tom used to drape over his knees and hung it on the velour chair to hide the printed ghost of his back and head. But in the silence of the empty rooms, his absence was everywhere. There was nowhere she could go to get away from it in this house that was all she had left of him. The black pit she used to sense lying beneath Tom now yawned just beneath the surface of her own days. She wondered if this was how her mother had felt when Dad died, all alone in the house they'd lived in together since before Mary was born. She'd never thought to ask, never imagined she could comfort a grief beyond her knowledge, beyond her desire to know. "Sorry, Mum," she whispered now. "Sorry I let you down. Sorry."

Vanessa Furse Jackson

She'd put on her coat and walk the streets until her legs were almost too weak to drag her home. She'd catch the bus out to the farm with the shop full of chickens and eggs and sausages, but she wouldn't get out when it stopped there. She'd wait in the empty bus until it turned around and came back into the town again. To begin with, she turned on the TV in the evenings, carefully avoiding *Coronation Street* and ballroom dancing, but her eyes would slide away from the raucous screen and range restlessly over the chair with its folded tartan rug, the urn on the mantelpiece, and the yellow canary that Tom had loved to hold until its china feathers grew warm in his hands. As spring gave way to summer, she found herself sitting in her chair for longer and longer periods in a thick, unbroken silence, waiting for Tom to tell her what to do. Until he did, everything, it seemed, must remain suspended. Even the clock on the sideboard was dumb. She no longer wound it, unable to bear the sound of its ticking.

Sara and Patrick watched the weeds grow in Man's garden. "Why doesn't she take care of it?" Sara fretted from the bedroom window.

"Because Man's not there any more," Patrick suggested.

"But she should keep it nice *because* he's not there any more," Sara said, not knowing quite what she meant.

"Like a memorial to him," said Patrick, who did know.

"How can she be so lazy? It looks awful, like she doesn't care about him now he's not here."

They watched her sidle out of the house in her long shapeless coat and scuttle to the bus stop or the corner shop or sometimes on down the long street of bricked terraced houses, walking until she disappeared from sight. "She's weird," Sara would say. "She is definitely weird."

"Poor old Mrs. Batty," Patrick said.

If they were outside and spotted her coming, they'd disappear as fast as they could, and the more times they did this, the more urgent it became to them to avoid her altogether.

"She doesn't *like* us," Sara said, when their mother told them of the offer of strawberries.

"She could *do* things to us," added Patrick.

"You silly children," their mother said, but they never did pick the strawberries. They watched from their bedroom window as the squirrels nipped off all the fruit and left piles of it between the rows to rot back into the ground. "They aren't eating the strawberries either," said Patrick.

"Animals know," said Sara.

They filled the notebook with everything they could remember about Man, planning what to include in low voices through the lengthening light of the evenings after they were supposed to be asleep in their beds. But when the book was finished, they were restless and not yet ready to let him go, still half afraid he would fade from them entirely.

"I know we have the book," Sara said, "and that's really good." School had ended for the summer, and Man should have been lying in his canvas chair in the sun, waiting for their visits.

"But we need something more," Patrick said.

"Something to remember him by."

"Something that was his, d' you mean?"

"Yes, but the witch 'd never let us have anything." Sara, cross-legged on her bed, stared furiously at the floor.

"Perhaps," Patrick said, in a voice that wondered at its daring, "we could find something of his for ourselves."

"How?" Sara demanded.

"When she's out."

"The canary," Sara breathed. "That's what he'd want us to have. Of course."

"Of course," Patrick echoed.

So one morning, they went to get it. They waited until their mother was busy on her computer and Mrs. Batsford had left her house with her old shopping bag on wheels, which meant she'd be at least half-an-hour wandering round Spar in her usual daze. Their friend the check-out lady had said to them it was like old Mrs. Batsford's mind had died along with her husband's body and what a crying shame it was, and the children had nodded sagely and said nothing.

They ran downstairs and into their back garden, climbed over the fence with the help of the wheelbarrow, and saw almost immediately that there was a small rectangle of window open at the back of the house. Within a couple of minutes, they were standing in the dimly lit living room that they hadn't been in since Man's death. Except . . . and Sara still shuddered at the image she couldn't shake from her mind of pongy Mrs. Batty sobbing wetly on her shoulder. "Ugh!" she said aloud, and Patrick put a comforting hand on her arm.

They stood in the doorway for a moment and looked around the room. It seemed to them greyer and more cave-like than ever. "It smells old," Patrick said.

"Like something died in here," Sara agreed.

They drew startled breaths, gulping with sudden laughter, and crept on into the room.

"His chair looks so empty," Sara said. She went over and stroked the tartan rug. "Yuck," she said, rubbing her fingers on her jeans. "It's all greasy."

"I don't like it in here," Patrick said. "And Man wouldn't like it in here." He went over to the mantelpiece and stood in front of it. "Look."

Sara joined him.

"What is it?" Patrick asked.

She could feel him trembling at her side. "I think it's him," she said.

"In there? All of him?"

"You burn down to very small pieces," Sara said. "To ash. To nothing."

"But on the mantelpiece," said the appalled Patrick. "Like an ornament."

"I suppose that's where you're meant to put it."

Patrick looked down at the empty chair then back again at the urn. "It's . . . it's horrible," he said.

"I wonder if she opens it and looks," Sara said.

"Don't!" Patrick said.

They gazed at the urn, both trying to recover a picture of the whistle-breathed, gentle Man with two clear tubes running out of his nose and his head resting against the high velour back of his chair.

"I'm glad he can't see it, aren't you?" Sara said.

"You mean see himself in it."

Sara put a finger up and touched the bronze-coloured urn. "It's plastic," she said, shocked. "Feel it. It's plastic."

"Not even real," Patrick said, putting his hands behind his back.

"Our Man isn't in there," Sara said, after a while. "He's gone somewhere else."

Patrick's fascinated gaze stayed on the plastic urn. "Can we go now?" he whispered.

Sara lifted the yellow canary off the mantelpiece, rubbed it on her T-shirt, kissed its head, and thrust it deep into her jeans pocket. "Mission accomplished," she said with satisfaction. There was a bird-shaped space left in the dust where it had sat, and she thought for a moment about trying to disguise it by cleaning the whole mantelpiece. "Forget it," she said. "She won't notice anyway. Let's scram."

Patrick, who had wanted to go, lingered. "Are we stealing?" he asked his sister. "Won't she mind?"

"We're taking the canary to the surface," Sara said. "We're the Safety Department. We're saving the poor bird from the bad air in this room and this house. Okay?"

"Okay," said Patrick. "I think."

When Mary saw the bird had gone, it didn't occur to her that they had taken it. She had no recollection of leaving a window open and anyway had no reason to connect the children with the bird. Tom had come and taken it back—she knew this at once. The canary mascot had saved neither him nor his younger brother, dead so many years ago from massive fibrosis of the lungs, and she found she wasn't sorry to see it gone. Yet her heart rejoiced that Tom, who had loved it, had taken the bird back as a sign to her. This, then, was what she'd been waiting for through the long months since he'd left her. She stood in front of the mantelpiece, still in the coat she'd put on to go shopping at the Spar Grocers, though it was really too hot for the July weather. She looked at the bird-shaped ghost in the dust, then at the urn. Her lips moved. "Where?" she asked.

"She's going back to the small colliery town outside Newcastle where her husband worked for so many years," the children's mother said. It was Saturday, and the family was having supper, the one meal of the week they always ate together.

Sara looked at Patrick, confident he would be thinking the same as she was: *she's trying to take him away from us, but she won't succeed. We have the canary, and we have him in the book forever.*

But Sara was wrong. Patrick, with a stone in his belly, was thinking, *we weren't kind, and he doesn't want to be with us any more.*

"She told me," said their father, "that wild horses wouldn't drag her up North again." He didn't sound very interested as he forked chicken pie into his mouth.

Vanessa Furse Jackson

"Perhaps she can't bear to be in the house where her parents and her husband died, poor old thing," said their mother, putting down her knife and fork with a sympathetic sigh.

"She's really moving house?" Sara said.

"Back to where he came from?" said Patrick.

"Quick pair, our kids, aren't they?" said their father, in tones of admiration that the children knew denoted the opposite.

"All the same," their mother mused, "it's odd she's moving. She always said this house was where she belonged. Where they used to live was dirty, she said. Coal dust on everything."

"No coal dust now," said their father. "The mines are all closed and the men all out of work. Long sterile job lines is all she'll find up there now. Pass the vino down this end, would you?"

"I wonder what happened to the canaries when they shut the mine," Sara said, her eyes bright.

"Being decent. That's what matters," Patrick half whispered.

Sara kicked him under the table. "I expect they let them go free, don't you?" she said.

Consequences

I.

Anna stared at the window of the Volvo, aware of dark banks and hedges rushing by but seeing only her shuttered, mutinous face biting down on recriminations.

"I'll pick you up at the station on Friday afternoon," Hal had said. "That way, I can get the cottage all warmed up and organized, and you won't have to do anything. I'll get food in, wood, coal, wine, whatever. Everything will be ready for you when you arrive. How's that sound?"

It had sounded like the old Hal. Excited, exciting, concerned to wrap her in layers of protection against the sharp edges of life she so often ran into.

The old Hal, offering to drive down with all the heavy luggage a couple of days before she could get off work, so that she wouldn't have to set up in a strange cottage, tired after a long journey. Kind Hal.

Their last chance, he'd said—to mend what had begun to crack so frighteningly and so fast.

And then he'd brought Jeremy with him.

Hot rage coiled in Anna's chest like serpents. Her shoulders were hunched tight and her neck was stiff from the angle at which she'd turned away from Hal. If he didn't grasp that she was upset, no, incensed by what he had done, then she didn't want to stay with the bastard anyway. She grimaced at her reflection, broken and framed by a steady rain that coursed down the glass.

Hal kept up a light flow of information, as a considerate host might to a guest newly arrived. But Anna noticed that Jeremy in the back seat said not a word, and when they arrived at the final turn-off to the cottage, it was Hal, after an awkward pause, who got out of the car to open the iron gate.

Abbot's Cottage had been lent to them by a friend of Hal's. Alone by a stream in a little wooded valley, secluded, thatched, old, it had sounded gloriously romantic, such a perfect setting for the undoing and remaking Anna had envisaged. No TV, no Internet, no phone. No more tangles— everything straight and true as it had been at the beginning.

The stoned track that plunged down between high trees might have enchanted Anna with its fairy remoteness from the hard city streets she trod daily, but she saw only how dark the air had become beneath the wet roof of leaves. She huddled close to the damp window as Hal negotiated a right-angled curve so sharp it almost had a front wheel over the bank. She didn't want to arrive—to have to uncurl and cope—but with one more steep run down, they were there, the engine stopped, the tick of cooling metal, the tinny rattle of a cock pheasant calling, rain on the roof of the car as they sat there for a moment in silence.

"Well, then," said Hal. "Here we are."

The cottage was indeed picture-book perfect with its heavy hood of thatch, its roses and clematis curling up a soft white exterior, deep-set windows, walls eighteen-inches thick. Beautiful. But small, Anna saw immediately. Tiny. A kitchen and a sitting-room downstairs, a bedroom and a bathroom upstairs—up stairs so steep she found herself climbing them on all fours.

"And just where does Jeremy think he's sleeping?" she hissed to Hal, as he ducked into the bedroom with her canvas tote bag and plunked it on the bed with a grunt. Even the double bed was small, she noted with disgust. The place was built for dwarves.

"Don't be so huffy, darling," Hal said. "The sofa in the sitting-room pulls down into a bed."

"Our last chance, you said," Anna cried. "And you've wrecked it before it's even begun. How could you?"

"Shh, he'll hear," said Hal.

"I don't *care*!"

"He needed a break—to get away. Really needed it. He's my little brother. What was I supposed to do? Say sorry, it's not convenient right now,

I'll look after you when I have time?" He turned away from her.

She felt a strong urge to hit him. "Yes, yes of course you should have. Aren't we more important?"

"Aren't you more important, you mean?" Hal, who had been staring out of the low window as if at an interesting view, swung around and went back to the door.

"You could have warned me. Given us the weekend together at least," Anna said. "But plotting behind my back—I'll never forgive you. Never!" She sat down on the edge of the bed and put her head down into her arms.

"I unpacked your things," he said, in that flat voice she hated. "They're in the wardrobe over there."

"Oh, what's the use?" Anna muttered into her sleeve.

"When you feel better," Hal said, and Anna knew by his restraint that she'd awoken his anger, "come downstairs and we'll have some tea—be civilized."

"Fuck you!" she shouted down the stairs after him.

After which little exhibition, she didn't feel that she could, with any dignity, go down again immediately. She went over to the window where Hal had stood. Through the water falling in bars off the thatch, she could see thin veils of rain blowing like smoke across the stream at the bottom of the garden. Beyond the hedge, a slab of green field reared up so steeply that she felt it might overbalance altogether and tumble forward onto the cottage, burying them here in a lonely, cloistered death. Little sky was visible, the field blocking what light there might be, as if deliberately shutting her off from discerning where she was. "This is a horrible place," she said, hoping Hal could hear her.

II.

As careful as he was in negotiating the treacherous stairs, Hal hit his head with a bang against the lintel of the door into the kitchen. "Jesus, that hurt," he said, slamming the door shut and reeling over to the kitchen table. "Damn stupid cottage—built for bloody midgets." He sat down, feeling for a moment as if he might vomit, not from concussion but from the tight coiling of anger held in physical check.

From the other side of the table, Jeremy looked at his brother morosely.

Vanessa Furse Jackson

"This was a big mistake all round, wasn't it?"

Hal swallowed, a hand pressed to his forehead.

"Why did I ever say I'd come?" Jeremy persisted. "I must have been off my head."

"Oh, for Christ's sake," Hal said. "Ouch."

"I feel like a human shield."

"You're damned ungrateful," Hal said, looking across at his brother with bloodshot eyes.

"Ungrateful? That's good, coming from you," Jeremy said.

"You wanted to come. Wanted to get away, you said. Remember all those holidays we had in Devon when we were kids?, you said."

"I thought it was you who asked me to come," Jeremy said. "To hold your hand."

"I brought you here because I thought you needed to get away," Hal said, getting up to fill the kettle at the sink. "And we had a damn good time last night, you said so yourself." He plugged in the kettle, switched it on, picked the teapot off the draining board, emptied the old leaves down the sink, swilled out the pot under the tap, dug a teaspoon into the opened packet of tea, and irritably slung in a couple of spoonfuls.

"I think I'll open a bottle of wine," Jeremy said.

"Goddammit!" Hal threw the teaspoon into the sink with such force that it spun around the stainless steel with orchestral violence, was flung out, and skidded across the tiled floor in a jangle of harsh notes.

Hal switched off the kettle and came and sat down. His nausea had gone. "She's not really as difficult as she's being right now," he said.

"I thought you told her I was coming," said Jeremy. "You told me you told her."

"I thought if there was a third person," Hal said. "She was making such a big deal of this weekend. Talking about last chances, getting melodramatic on me. I hate showdowns. Scenes."

"I don't know Anna," Jeremy said. "I have no idea what she feels about this weekend, or about you, and certainly not what she feels about me. Except I sense it's nothing good."

"What d'you mean, you don't know Anna?" Hal asked. He touched his forehead gingerly and winced. "We've been married for seven years."

"You and she have been married for seven years," Jeremy said.

"So of course you know her."

"I came to your wedding. We were all at Dad's funeral. I came to dinner at your place once. I don't know Anna."

"Is that all?" Hal asked, deflated. "Well, I'm sorry. How time flies. Good thing you and I manage all those lunches, then."

"Nothing to be sorry about," Jeremy said, getting up to find the wine. "Long boozy lunches do me fine, big brother. Just you and me and the Pinot Noir. No complications. Fine and dandy with me."

"Not that boozy," Hal said, defensively. "Good lunches. Good food, good talk."

"Boozy," Jeremy said, pulling out the cork. "You and me, just look at us. Look at last night."

"What about last night? We had a good time, didn't we?"

"Thought the Volvo was never to going to make the hairpin bend, you drunken sod. How many rounds did you buy?"

"Nice pub, that," Hal said, grinning. "Don't tell Anna."

"Oh, the tangled webs we weave," Jeremy sighed, bringing the bottle and two glasses to the table. He sat down. "Here's to us, then, mate. Cheers."

"Cheers."

They drank.

III.

When Anna came downstairs, she had changed from the well-tailored work suit in which she had travelled to an oversized sweatshirt over fleecy joggers and was prepared to relax her position perhaps a fraction, though she still felt Hal owed her an apology. But finding the kitchen deserted, the kettle full but cold, and the teapot coated inside with tea-leaves that were half dry and half sodden from residual water, her sense of grievance revived. She could hear the other two in the sitting-room next door, laughing, of all things. She swilled out the pot, plugged in the kettle, made herself a mug of tea from a tea bag, and sat down to drink it at the kitchen table, hoping that her movements would bring Hal in to find her. She listened to the conversation murmuring through the thick old walls, but she couldn't detect what they were saying. The only distinct sound was that intermittent laughter. Despondently, she reflected that they were almost certainly talking

Vanessa Furse Jackson

about her.

When Hal came in for another bottle of wine, she had nearly finished the tea. "There you are," he said. "I didn't hear you come down. Feeling better?"

"Yes, thanks," she said, blowing across the top of her almost empty mug.

"That's a good girl," Hal said, coming round and giving her a quick hug. She squeezed him back, relieved at his affability, irritated by his patronizing tone.

"What are you sitting here in the gloom for?" he asked, flipping on the overhead light.

Anna blinked.

"Thought we'd have a bit of wine," he said, lifting a bottle out from a box behind her and taking another glass from the sideboard. "Come and join us next door. We've got a nice little fire going."

Reluctantly, Anna got up and followed him into the sitting-room, half-nodding to Jeremy who was sitting, she noticed, in the one armchair in the room. She sat down on the rather frayed sofa-bed, choosing the end that was farthest away from him and trying not to think of him sleeping on it last night. She stared into the fire, though there wasn't much to see. Every so often a spiral of smoke would escape the lip of the mantel and scurry up the discoloured wall above the fireplace, but the pale flames were clearly struggling for survival.

Hal opened the bottle of wine with a bright popping of cork that seemed to mock the tension in the room. He poured wine for the three of them with extreme concentration, caught himself about to say 'cheers' and sat down quietly on the edge of the sofa, closer physically to his brother than to his wife. He sighed.

Her presence, Anna realized resentfully, had put a damper on the previous flow of conversation. "How nice to have a fire," she said to Hal, thinking, come on, you bastard, this is your party.

"Nothing like a good open fire," Hal replied, as if he was an encouraging uncle instead of her husband. He leant forward and poked hopefully at the smoking logs.

"We heard you come down," Jeremy said, "but we thought you might be wanting to be on your own for a while, so we didn't disturb you." He smiled hopefully, as if waiting for a pat or a tidbit, Anna thought.

She didn't look directly at him or at Hal. She stared into the fire, cradling her glass as if it were her mug of tea and then drinking it in thirsty gulps.

"Another round?" said Hal, leaping up to oblige. "Goodness, and I need to open a bottle to go with supper."

"What are we eating?" Anna asked.

They ate ham and cheese sandwiches with chutney and pickled onions out of a jar, followed by chunks of fruit and nut chocolate, and the conversation slowly warmed. The chicken and broad beans and baby carrots and new potatoes that Hal had bought for Anna to cook remained idle and raw, Hal having assured her that although he'd got something special for tomorrow, he'd been sure she wouldn't want to cook on her first night, so please, if she wouldn't mind just sandwiches in the kitchen.

Jeremy, with fond recollections of the hot and spicy pheasant pie he and Hal had devoured in the local pub last night, washed down his pickled onions with drafts of vin de table and watched Hal and Anna get to the point where they could touch each other without apologizing. Anna watched Hal and Jeremy performing their brother act for her. Hal, relieved at feeling back in control of himself and the situation, watched Anna and Jeremy, wishing they would relax and make friends. And gradually, as they sat in the kitchen, elbows on the table, passing the wine to and fro, the knots began to loosen until at last they felt it safe to go back and sit by the fire.

IV.

"Well, I think it's about time to turn in," said Hal, stretching theatrically and standing up from the sofa where he'd been sitting with his arm around Anna. He had squeezed her shoulder before he stood up, so she knew quite well what this comparatively early move towards bed meant. She found herself both embarrassed and reluctant to comply, with Jeremy so studiously keeping his gaze turned to the fire and Hal so sure she would fall in with his plans. "You go," she said. "I'll be up in a moment. I can't bear to waste this fire." And indeed, the fire was now as willing as earlier it had been sullen, flame and smoke rushing obediently up the chimney and sending out such a radiant heat that they'd had to open the window.

"Perhaps Jeremy might like his bedroom back," Hal said, and the chill in

Vanessa Furse Jackson

his voice awoke a familiar perversity in Anna.

"Too hot," Jeremy said. "I'll have to let it burn down a bit before I turn in. Sleep well, big brother." He didn't look up.

"Well, then," Hal said, looming over them, his head almost touching the ceiling so that his shadow filled one wall as a giant's might. "See you in the morning, then, Jerry." He turned stiffly and left the room as if Anna were no longer there.

"He calls you *Jerry?*" Anna said, as they listened to the alarming creaks of Hal climbing the stairs. He would want to talk in bed—to probe the day, to show his displeasure at her behaviour—and after she had cried he would want to make love. She didn't think she had the energy to face the role in which she'd been cast. If she waited for a bit, perhaps he'd be asleep when she went up.

"It's what he calls me when he wants to remind me that he's older than I am," Jeremy said. "That he has rights I don't."

"I see," said Anna.

They listened to the faint sound of the lavatory flushing upstairs, water running away.

"Amazingly soundproof, these old cottages," Jeremy said.

"Yes."

Hal's footsteps overhead, muffled but distinct. Then silence.

Anna listened to the rain pattering outside the window, to the gurgle of the stream at the bottom of the garden. "I should go up," she said.

"Don't," Jeremy said. "I wanted to say something to you."

She looked across at him, noticing, not for the first time, how similar his eyes were to Hal's, though the rest of him was quite different.

"I wanted to say I was sorry," Jeremy went on.

Different, how? Younger? Finer, somehow.

"For butting in on your weekend like this."

Leaner, sharper-boned. "Butting in?" she said.

"Playing gooseberry. I wouldn't have come if I'd known."

"What?"

"That this weekend was to be . . . you know. Hal didn't tell me."

"Tell you what?" Anna asked, wanting evidence of Hal's duplicity but wanting also to keep Jeremy talking until she'd worked out the teasing likeness/difference between him and Hal.

"That you were seeing it as a . . ." Be careful now, Jeremy thought.

"As a what?"

"As a last chance was I think what he said you said."

"What you think he said I said. How interesting," Anna said, thinking, what a *shit*.

"He said, she said," and Jeremy laughed suddenly.

"Oh, Consequences," Anna said, and blushed.

The two brothers had elected to play Consequences after supper when they discovered that Anna had never played it before. Actually, she realized after they started that she had played it as a child—it was the game she remembered as the verbal version of Heads, Bodies and Tails. But she didn't then confess to Hal and Jeremy that she knew the game. It was more fun to let them teach her, vying with each other as to who could make her, but primarily themselves, laugh the most. Everything had gone well for several rounds, in the predictable vein of 'Martin Amis met The Queen in the cupboard under the stairs'—much funnier to those playing the game than to anyone else—until, all of them beginning to push closer the edge, Hal had unpeeled his sheet of paper and read,

Jeremy Fisher

Met:

The Sleeping Beauty

At:

The Gingerbread Cottage in the Dark Woods

He said to her:

"I lust."

She said to him:

"It will have to be at night."

And the consequence was:

They never found their way home again.

Innocuous, surely, but there had been an odd little pause after he read it, and he failed to find anything to say quickly enough to cover up the fact that no one was laughing. Anna, knowing she had written the third and sixth lines, was trying to remember which way round the paper had gone. Jeremy, who knew quite well he had started this consequence, was hoping his message had reached Anna. They didn't play any more rounds.

"Poor Hal," Jeremy said now. "He must be wishing he'd never brought

Vanessa Furse Jackson

me with him."

But suddenly, Anna was glad that Jeremy was here—glad to be talking to him in this cottage in the woods before a leaping fire—glad to have this younger Hal to fence with. *That was it.* Blood coursed giddily up her neck and into her face, and she looked over at Jeremy to find him staring intently at her. She wanted to look away, but she was caught by this answer to her riddle. Not physical likeness exactly, but the same vibration, atmosphere, spark as when she and Hal were first together.

Jeremy smiled at her giveaway blush and the arrested brightness in her eyes, and his heart started thumping nervously. He wanted to touch her, to put his arm around her as Hal had and feel what Hal felt as she leant into his body. Nothing more. He came over and sat beside her on the sofa. "Do you remember," he said casually, "the day you and I walked through Kensington Gardens talking about the Rossetti exhibition?"

"The Morris exhibition," Anna said. "At the Tate, wasn't it?"

"And then we got on to Pre-Raphaelite poetry."

"All that effete chivalry."

"You liked Christina Rossetti. That's what I was remembering."

"And daffodils. How did we get on to daffodils?"

"You wouldn't let me kiss you goodbye," Jeremy said.

"How ice maiden of me," Anna said and found she was crying, and then that she was crying with Jeremy's arms around her.

"Don't, Anna, don't," he said. "Please don't be unhappy." And as she leant into him, he began to stroke her back. She found it extraordinarily soothing.

"Hal and I could read each other's minds once, we were so close," Anna said after a while, "and now we can't talk about anything."

"You talked this evening," Jeremy said, handing her his handkerchief.

"Not about anything important."

"The seven-year itch?" he said lightly.

"He's not like he used to be. He gets so angry with me. I'm not even sure he cares about me any more." Anna blew her nose.

"I'm sure he does," Jeremy said, thinking, then why don't you give her to me, mate?

"I used to feel comforted by him. Also exhilarated," she said. "Has he changed? Have I? Why do people change?"

"He still loves you. He told me," Jeremy said, feeling exhilarated himself.

"He did?"

"Yes, he did. So stop thinking about it."

"He's never been violent, but sometimes I wonder," Anna said, brooding.

"Hal? Never."

"He can be such a bastard."

"What you need is to let me take your mind off your worries for a while," Jeremy said.

"You are so like Hal," she said sleepily.

"Oh, thanks very much," Jeremy said, but she could feel him laughing.

"No," she said. "I mean you're so like him when I first met him and everything was exciting. I have missed that so much."

I wonder if she knows what she's saying, Jeremy thought.

And Anna, closing her eyes and moving her body within his embrace, allowed herself for a brief moment to believe she'd gone back in time. In a minute, I will go up to bed, she thought.

When he put a hand, feather light, between her legs, she was breathing so evenly that he wondered at first if she had indeed fallen asleep.

"I must go up," she said eventually, getting to her feet and making a great show of stretching and yawning. "Hal will be wondering where I am."

"You're not really going?" Jeremy said.

"Dear Jeremy," she said. "You know I must. Good night and . . ." She stopped herself saying thanks for everything, adding instead, "Sleep well," which she realized afterwards was no better. She bent down and kissed him. "Dear Jeremy," she said again, and left.

He listened to her climb the stairs. "Bitch," he said.

V.

Next morning when they awoke, it was to a clear sky, the sun shining so benignly on the slab of field beyond the cottage that the hill seemed to be lying back at a gentler angle that it had the day before. Looking out of the bedroom window, Anna could see Jeremy, a small figure at the top of the hill, looking down at the cottage. She waved before turning back to Hal.

"Come on, lazybones," she said. "It's a glorious day."

Hal grunted and rolled over onto his back. He wanted to ask her why she'd had a bath when she came up to bed last night. Just to see what she'd say. "I had a lousy night's sleep," he said. "This bed is the pits."

"You were sleeping like a baby when I came in," Anna said. She wasn't sure if this was true, but he certainly hadn't said anything as she had slid in beside him, trying to take up the least room possible. And then she must have slept.

"What were you and Jeremy talking about after I left?" Hal asked.

"Good heavens, I don't know," said Anna. "Too much wine. I don't remember. Nothing very important, anyway." With a sudden jolt, she became aware that the window she had just looked out of was wide open, as had been the sitting-room window, directly below, last night. "We didn't disturb you, did we?" she said.

Hal lay with his eyes closed, remembering the murmur of their talk drifting upward against the soft rain. He hadn't heard what they were saying—hadn't really paid attention until the voices stopped. It was the consequent silence that had alerted him. He had lain, every muscle tense, listening in a darkness that had seemed to press against the skin of his face. "Your talking didn't disturb me," he said. He knew only too well how quiet she could be—knew how much it turned her on to pretend she wasn't aroused.

Had they made any noise?, Anna wondered. She was sure they hadn't. She had been so careful to give nothing away. "You're not jealous, are you?" she said, coming over and sitting on the bed. Better to be completely straightforward.

"What happened, Anna?" Hal asked, opening his eyes.

"You've got a bruise on your forehead," she said. "When did you do that?"

"What happened with Jeremy?"

"Nothing," she said. "Why are you asking?"

"I wanted us to be all right," Hal said quietly. "And we're not, you can see we're not. We're a mess." He sounded close to tears.

"Don't say that, Hal, please don't." She willed him to turn cold, angry—that, she could cope with. She felt panicky.

"You and he . . ." His voice broke against the graphic picture in his mind.

"No," she said.

"You did, didn't you?" he said.

"No. Did what?"

"With Jeremy."

"No, I didn't. I didn't sleep with your brother, you have to believe me. I love you, Hal. And I want us to be all right, too, really all right—like we were at the beginning." She broke into noisy sobs at the truths of these statements and flung herself down on the bed across Hal's body.

VI.

The cottage looked very small from the top of the hill. When she had waved, she'd looked like a stick figure leaning out of a dolls-house. Soft, warm Anna. She had lain so quiet in his arms last night, so still. When, eventually, he'd gone out into the garden to pee, he'd listened beneath their bedroom window in the dark. Hearing nothing but an intense silence, he'd tortured himself by imagining her in Hal's arms, as quiet, as still. But slippery as a silver fish. When she had come to climax, it was with so light a flickering against him that he might have missed it had he not felt also the burn of the flush that swept through her, seen the small shudder of her mouth. He'd not shown her that he knew, though, and when she'd let him continue on for a moment or two, he had been so sure, so *grateful*. And then she had stood up, pulling down her sweatshirt as if nothing at all had happened, and said, I must go up. I must go up. Just like that. Did she really think that he would think nothing had happened? "*Dear* Jeremy," he said aloud, mocking the ache in him that wouldn't be stilled. "And just what do I say to big brother Hal? Let sleeping beauties lie?"

VII.

In the car going to the station, Hal insisted that Jeremy sit in the front with him. "You don't mind, do you, darling?" he said cheerfully to Anna, as if arranging the children. "You'll get to sit up front on the way back, but this is poor old Jerry's last chance."

"Of course I don't mind," she said, glad not to have Jeremy staring at

Vanessa Furse Jackson

the back of her neck all the way. He'd returned to the cottage just as she and Hal had climbed down the steep little stairs into the kitchen, and his eyes had followed her uncomfortably all through breakfast. She sensed he knew that she and Hal had just made love, and she wanted to apologize to him for last night, but she wasn't sure if he'd known or not that she'd actually come—which she hadn't meant to—and if he hadn't known—she'd been so careful—then perhaps it was best just to let things lie. So she'd eaten her boiled egg with delicate concentration and listened to Jeremy telling Hal he'd had to go up the hill to make his phone work and he was terribly sorry to cut things so short, but something urgent had come up that he'd have to take care of before Monday, all of which she was grateful to believe.

And now Hal was chatting lightly to Jeremy in the front of the car as he'd chatted to her on the journey yesterday. Jeremy, the honoured guest, to be politely speeded on his way. Anna felt quite sorry for him.

"Sorry you couldn't stay longer," Hal was saying. "If it keeps fine, I'd thought of running over to the coast later on this morning, finding a pub that serves local fish."

"Anna doesn't like fish," Jeremy said.

"Yes, I do," she said from the back seat, surprised that he'd known. Had she told him?

"And we really ought to pick up some cider while we're here," Hal went on.

"Lethal stuff, cider," Jeremy said.

"Yes," said Hal. "My God, yes. Do you remember Dad giving it to us on that holiday in Combe Martin?"

"You never know what's going to happen when you allow someone to drink too much," Jeremy said in a level voice.

"Sick as dogs, we were. Dear, oh dear."

"Some people," Jeremy continued, "aren't so much sick as set free."

"Yes, that's very true," said Hal. "Do the most extraordinary things under the influence. I remember . . ."

"Or allow the most extraordinary things to be done to them," said Jeremy.

In the back seat, Anna gritted her teeth.

"I remember taking all my clothes off once," Hal said.

"There's that, too," said Jeremy.

"In a bar, I think. Where were we, Anna?"

"Corfu, if it's our honeymoon you're remembering," Anna said, thinking, take that, *Jerry*.

"Lord, yes, so it was. I don't think I've done anything quite as outrageous since." Hal laughed.

"Perhaps you should," Jeremy said, still in that polite, even voice.

"You wouldn't want to see me like that again, would you, Anna?"

"Oh, I don't know," she said, remembering the crazy electricity of those two weeks. The way he could turn her on by just looking at her. Like Jeremy had last night. She flushed, saw Hal looking at her in the rearview mirror, coughed.

"Anna needs a bit of outrageousness," Jeremy said, as if he was discussing the stock market. "Or outrage."

"Isn't the countryside looking lovely this morning?" Hal said, opening his window. "That too cold for you, darling? Just say if it is."

"No, I like the fresh air," Anna said, grateful for the fragrant wind on her cheeks, thinking how like Hal Jeremy was in his anger.

"Gorgeous clouds coming in from the south-west. Like great swans," Hal said.

"Nice weather for the time of year," Jeremy agreed.

At the station, the only parking spot they could find was down a distant side street, and Anna hoped that Jeremy would just hop out and go—no fond farewells on the station platform. But Hal, still playing the perfect host, insisted on going with him to ensure he got off safely. Anna, left in the car by her own choice, moved into the front seat, which was warm from Jeremy's body, and began to worry.

She needn't have. Jeremy was angry with her, not with Hal, he discovered when he was alone with his brother. He felt sorry for him, in fact, which rather surprised him. He thought he'd always envied him.

"Anything wrong?" Hal asked abruptly, as they stood looking down the platform at the rails curving out of sight.

"I told you I shouldn't have come," Jeremy said.

"Last night," Hal said.

"You don't need anyone to hold your hand."

"You and Anna," Hal said.

"We didn't, if that's what you mean," Jeremy said.

Vanessa Furse Jackson

"Oh," Hal said.

The train came.

VIII.

So in the end, it was in the Volvo on a hard city street that the last chance, the showdown that Hal and Anna had travelled to a sequestered cottage in Devon to stage, took place.

"Well, that's done," Hal said, getting back into the car and shutting his door firmly. He put on his seatbelt, pushed the key into the ignition, and sat there in silence.

Anna turned to him. "He caught the train all right, then?" she said.

"Yes."

"Look," they both began at the same time.

"Sorry," they both said.

"You first," Hal said.

Anna composed herself. "Sometimes I feel," she said, "as if you don't really love me any more." She waited. "There's a note in your voice."

"I don't mean it to be there," Hal said. But he knew what she meant— she did exasperate him. Sometimes she enraged him.

"You shut me out," she said. "You put me some place behind you where I won't be in your way."

"I don't," he said, appalled by the truth of what she was saying. There were times when he had to put a shield up between her and the anger she awoke in him. Last night, for instance. He unclipped his seatbelt so he could look at her more easily.

"That's what it feels like, anyway," she said. "Being shut out."

Without a shield, he was sometimes afraid he might lash out and hit her. "But I do love you," he said. And that was true, too, he thought.

"Do you?" she asked.

"There are times," he said, "when I'm not sure if you're telling me the truth or not. Or all of the truth." But he wouldn't really hit her, would he?

"I wouldn't lie to you," she said. "I wouldn't. Not about anything important."

"Were you drunk last night?" he asked.

"You made me think of our honeymoon," she said. "All that talk about drinking."

"God, we were young," he said.

"I wish it could be that time again," she said. "When everything was so magical. Cinderella and her stupid prince had nothing on us. I wish . . ."

"But now is now, darling," Hal reminded her gently. "We can't go back and be those people again. Taking my clothes off in a bar, for Christ's sake. This is marriage, not, not . . ."

"Romance."

"It's for life," Hal said, wondering if he really meant that. That was the trouble with talking about this kind of thing—words created certainties you weren't sure about.

"But, oh, I loved the romance," Anna said, leaning over onto his shoulder and burying her head in his familiar smell. She thought, he still loves me the same as he always has.

And he thought, I'll make a pledge never be angry with her again. He put his arm around here, and they sat content for the moment, at peace.

"Love in a parked car," she said. "How romantic." And laughed.

"Romance is what you make of it," Hal said. "Let's get some champagne to go with supper tonight."

"Oh, Hal," Anna said, a sudden memory of Jeremy's feather light touch making her heart race. "Yes, please." She sat up eagerly and moved back into her seat.

Hal put on his seatbelt again and started the car.

He said to her, "I won't shut you out any more."

She said to him, "And I promise I will always, always tell you the truth."

The Stand-In

I haven't spoken to anyone but my mother for a year now. Really spoken, I mean. I've said "Thank you" to the man who cuts my hair and to the woman behind the Post Office grille. I don't speak to the check-out girls in the supermarket. They are too offhand to merit expressions of gratitude that I don't feel.

I suppose I may occasionally have said "Good morning" to a neighbour in the street. Old habits die hard. But Mummie is the only person with whom I can have the kind of discussions I revel in on those long dark evenings before the fire in the sitting-room. I am a lucky, lucky man.

We got rid of the television set. I took the wretched thing to the city's Household Waste Recycling Centre. I don't need any reminders of my former life. But we still listen to the radio. Never news, which can only depress. Weather, sometimes. *Woman's Hour*, to which my mother is devoted, and *Desert Island Discs* if there's anyone intelligent on. Sometimes a concert if I'm ironing clothes or polishing the furniture and need some company while I'm doing so. And we still have my old record player, though I fear the needle is getting very worn now, so we save my small collection of records for special occasions. We like a quiet house, Mummie and I.

She taught me never to sit with idle hands, so I continue to embroider and do *gros point* needlework for the cathedral. "You have such neat hands, James," she will say. "I do believe your stitches are smaller and more even than my own." She has always been so generous to me, my mother. The Cathedral sends me mitres and copes, tippets and scapulars that need careful mending, and I design and execute hassocks and altar cloths on commission. It brings in a tiny income, and I can do all my business by post, which is as

I prefer it these days. I keep busy enough. There's always something to do around the house.

My father used to say that he'd work until the day he died, and that is what Mr. Joyless did. The site of the premises from which he ran his little optician's business in the High Street is currently occupied by an Italian espresso bar, which I expect enrages him from his cold plot in the graveyard of St. Pius and St. Philip. He loathed the merest whiff of anything foreign.

Father wanted me to follow him into the business, and throughout my childhood he expected me to accompany him to the shop on Saturday mornings, when he opened from nine until one o'clock. I liked trying on the empty spectacle frames, catching sight of myself in the mirrored backs behind the shelves, looking exotic in tortoise-shell or flying wings of sequins. But his eye would grow cold if he caught me doing this, and I despised the tedious hours spent learning to re-shape ear pieces, fit lenses, tighten those miniscule screws, flatter the puffy women who sat before their own reflections exclaiming, "And to think I used to have perfect eyesight." Adding to my small pale self, "You don't know how lucky you are to be young." I never felt lucky when I was young.

When, in defiance of his narrow-minded parochialism, I went to London to become a dresser in the theatre, my father waited for the phase to pass, unsmiling but certain I would be home again soon with the proverbial tail between my legs. When I became, for a considerably increased salary, a stand-in at that great bastion of British cinema, the Rank Organisation, he told me I would be welcome in his house only at Christmas and for my mother's birthday, this last a grudging concession to her feelings. He would be happy, he said, never to see me again. I have to say the sentiment was mutual. I loathed every living and dying cell in my father's body.

I bought a small flat in Amersham, near to the studios and easy enough for my mother to reach by train. So it was that she began to come and stay with me, feeling, she laughed, exactly as if she was conducting an illicit affair behind my father's back. "I don't tell him I am coming to you," she said. "I just say it's time for one of my restorative weekends. And he gives me the train fare and asks me what I have left him to eat in the fridge." I longed to suggest arsenic casserole, but I still thought in those days that she was fond of him, and I had no desire to hurt her. I wished him dead, but I also wished myself born of a union that had been consummated in harmony.

Vanessa Furse Jackson

Incompatible desires, you might think, but I couldn't bear the idea that she might have been coerced into an unhappy marriage—into conceiving a child she didn't want by a man she couldn't love. I have my pride.

I used to take her dancing. I wonder if one can still do that. Probably not, unless you count the un-partnered gymnastics that pass for dancing these days. You're a solo act on the dance floor or you're a duo having sex, as far as I can see. There no longer seems to be the subtle in between—the *frisson*—of touching your dancing partner *just so*, while never overstepping the bounds of decorum. I took Mummie to the local Palais on Saturday nights, where if we were lucky there was a live dance band, but, if not, always the recorded music of her youth: Glenn Miller, Benny Goodman, Hutch, the Savoy Salon Orchestra. I bought her dresses, yards of chiffon and tulle, which she kept at my flat, and we whirled the floor in waltzes and foxtrots and tangos. Oh, the tangos. She had a figure like a girl's then and the most divinely blonde curls. I loved the feel of her curved back, the muscles moving under my hand, her gay smile, the fragrance she wore, *L'Air du Temps*. If I shut my eyes, I can bring our perfect partnership to life in vivid technicolour. On the studio floor, I was always a stand-in. On the dance floor, in her arms, I was the star, fêted and brave.

For years, each weekend followed the same pattern. She'd arrive by train on Saturday morning, and we'd talk until lunch-time. After the meal, she'd rest on her bed in the spare room I decorated and kept immaculate just for her. She'd smoke her cigarettes and read or doze for the afternoon, tired to death, I used to think, from her ordeal of a life with my fish-eyed father. Later, there would be tea and then the fun of dressing up to go out. A light dinner, dancing. Oh yes, indeed—I have only to summon the memory, and we are dancing together like Rogers and Astaire, my beloved Mummie and I.

On Sundays, we were sad because in the afternoon she must catch her train back to the house I'd known all my life and in which I was no longer welcome. Before she left, we'd walk together on the common. "I wish you didn't have to go," I'd say. "I wish you'd stay with me always."

"You know I must go, James," she'd reply, with a little squeeze of my hand, and that would be that. I admired and envied her courage more than I can say.

She was the only person I knew who called me James. My father called me Jim for as long as I can remember, as if by calling me Jim he could create the solid workaday son he wanted, not the alien changeling he'd mistakenly produced. To my father, I was never more than a poor substitute. At the studios, I was Jimmie, nicely reduced in stature. Jimmie, do this—Jimmie, do that. Stand here. Stand there. Disappear now, Jimmie.

I prefer James. James has dignity.

Had I possessed my mother's courage, I'd have become an actor, as I dreamed of doing for so long. I thought if I worked in a theatre, immersed myself in the world of theatre, I'd somehow assume the mantle of an actor in the natural way of things. I dressed for a lovely gentleman when I started, and I don't use the word lightly. A real gentleman, courteous, kind, and *simpatico* to my unexpressed longing to follow him out onto the lighted set beyond the wings where I waited for his exits and entrances.

One night, when an unimportant actor playing a servant was ill, he arranged for me to join the crowd scene at the banquet during which Banquo's Ghost appears to Macbeth. After I'd dressed him in Macbeth's soldier's garb for the start of the show, he dressed me as a serving boy, smoothing the rouge onto my cheekbones with his own hands, and laughing as he did so. "Won't they all be surprised?" he said. "But when they ask me about it, I shall say, 'Serving boy? What serving boy?'"

The play proceeded. I got him changed into his courtly robes and stood shivering at the side of the stage upon which I'd yearned to tread. But long before he'd sent the murderers to kill Banquo, I'd had to run to the lavatory to be sick, my guts in merciless spasms of terror. I was miserable, utterly humiliated. My gentleman just shrugged when I confessed. I could tell he was disappointed his little jape hadn't come off, but he didn't say anything. I can still remember the feel of his hands smoothing the rouge onto my face and then the fear coursing through me like poison. I hadn't thought of myself as a coward up until then. It's not a nice feeling, not nice at all.

I put the theatre behind me after that little *débâcle* and discovered that I felt much more at home in the film studios. I had my position as a stand-in for the very top people, Rank's stars and starlets, which put me far above the extras who just stood around waiting for their little scraps of scene to happen. People knew me there, knew I could be relied upon. Hold it there, Jimmie. Don't move till we've measured, Jimmie. Thanks, Jimmie, good job. I was always a professional, and I never again made the mistake of venturing into the limelight. Better to blend into the shadows—to become expert at the art of effacement, representing the body of someone other than myself, whose skin I would never be called upon to inhabit. There were regrets, a few, since you ask. But we are who we are, *faute de mieux*.

And I had the delicious weekends to look forward to, when Mummie could escape her confines and come to live with me in my flat in Amersham that no one but she ever saw. How long ago it seems since we danced to "String of Pearls" and "Chantanooga Choo Choo," and yet, as the film shows again in my mind, how tangibly I can feel her body leaning into mine, responsive to the lightest pull as we sweep around the corners of the sprung oak dance floor, dodging the other couples, laughing at our effortless expertise. She was eighteen years older than I. She might have been my twin. She was far more my soul-mate than she was my cold brute of a father's.

Once in my youth, on a Saturday morning at my father's shop, a young girl of about my own age, fourteen or so, came in to choose the frames for her first pair of glasses. Her heavyset mother was with her, and she and my father colluded together to persuade the girl that the occasion was an important rite-of-passage, a step towards the mysteries of womanhood, as if buying glasses should be viewed as a special treat. I had watched my father perform this fawning ritual so many times that I could have played his part myself.

"Now, this pair really brings out your eyes."

"You see, dear, I told you it wouldn't be so bad."

"If I might just draw your hair back like so—quite sophisticated, hmmm? Or perhaps you'd like to try these. The frames pick up the colour of your skin remarkably, if you don't mind my saying so."

"Oh, I like those, Elspeth."

"Now these are a little dearer—a French designer—but I think you'll agree they enhance your looks quite dramatically. Yes, I thought so. They might have been made for you."

"Oh, look at those, Elspeth."

"If you'd just tilt your head up a bit. There. An amazing fit. Perfect."

But they weren't perfect. Elspeth knew it, and so did I. The glasses made her look plain. They took away the youth and freshness, which was all the beauty she had, and put a mask of premature adulthood—of her cow-like mother—on her small features. I could sense her misery, her despair at being forced into choosing, or having chosen for her, the means whereby she would be forever marked *unattractive*.

"Don't you think so, Jim? This is my son, Jim. Jim knows almost as much about the business as I do."

I knew my part in the ritual. I had said it often enough: yes, those are perfect, perfect, yes, they really look good on you. I glanced, embarrassed, into Elspeth's bespectacled, swimming eyes, and I said, "I think they look awful, as a matter of fact. Glasses don't suit her at all."

Elspeth tore off the pair of French frames and burst into tears. I caught my father's eye in the mirror, blazing in a pinched face, and knew I'd committed an unforgivable crime.

"Well!" said the cow.

"I knew it," sobbed Elspeth. "I'm a freak. I told you so. I told you."

"Would you leave us now, please, Jim?" my father said, meaning, wait for me in my office until I have finished with these good people and have time to come and give you the thrashing of your life.

I went and waited for my beating in the cold, windowless office with the paraffin heater that he never lit and the metal ruler with which he would beat me lying cold and sleek in his desk drawer. My heart was drubbing in my chest, and I swore to myself that this time I wouldn't cry, even though I knew I would, not at the pain but at the anger that would stream from my father like flames to shrivel my very soul. My demon father. But I was glad I'd done what I did and a little amazed at my temerity. I am still a little amazed.

"Why did you do it?" my mother asked later, tenderly stroking my hair as I lay in my bed on my front.

"He's a bully," I said, still teary.

Her hand stilled for a moment. "A bully?"

"He was making her accept what he wanted," I said, from the muffling folds of my pillow. "Not what she wanted. She could have been me."

"Oh, my dear," Mummie said. "You mustn't stand up to him. You really mustn't. You're not strong enough, little James."

Although unspoken, it was accepted after that incident that I wouldn't be following my father into the optician's business.

I enjoyed my work with Rank for the most part. I liked the variety of the different settings and actors and directors, and I liked the constancy and

Vanessa Furse Jackson

camaraderie of the people who worked as I did behind the scenes, year after year, film after film. I never made any close friends—I didn't need to. I had Mummie, you see. But we had plenty of laughs together, us old timers at the studios, and a reputation, well-earned, for professional excellence. It was a happy place to work, a good life, whatever my father thought.

But all good things must come to an end, and for me the end began one weekend about . . . my word, it must be almost ten years ago now. *Tempus fugit*, indeed.

Mummie had come up to Amersham for a restorative weekend, one of the very few she'd managed that particular year, as my father was getting increasingly resentful of her being away from home. Late on the Saturday afternoon, she came out from her rest looking more tired than I'd seen her for a long time and said quite suddenly, "It's becoming impossible, James. Your father. We may not be able to do this for very much longer."

I was filled with terror, flooded. "Not do this?" I said. "What do you mean? Not do what?"

"I may not be able to come and stay with you here any more," she said, sitting wearily on my couch and patting the place next to her.

"But Mummie," I said, and I know my voice was shaking, "you're all I have. How can you not come to see me any more?" I sat beside her as she'd indicated, putting my hands between my thighs and gripping them there, a habit I have when I'm particularly upset. I have distressingly weak insides.

She sighed, a deep sigh, as if she was straining at the far end of a tether that had been cruelly attached to her by we-both-knew-who. "He never asked," she said, and put her arm around me. "He still never asks. But while I am gone, he goes to the shop and spends his time there until I return."

"So?" I said. "Let him, if he wants to be there."

"I've been thinking about it all afternoon," she said. "He doesn't eat what I leave him. I don't think he eats at all."

Staring at her averted profile, I could see her grey roots beneath the brave blonde rinse. She can't become old, I thought in a panic.

She went on, "He stays away from the empty house, sleeps in that horrid office at the shop, then comes to meet me at the station unshaven and silent."

I took a moment to process this unattractive picture. "Is he"—I asked this with some care—"Is he quite sane?"

She sighed again. "I'm his wife," she said. "To have and to hold in sickness and in health. I would never abandon him, James."

I thought of his abandonment of me, his only child. I thought of his cold eye, his scorching anger, his indifference to my feelings. "Come and live here," I urged her. "Come and live with me. I'd make you so happy, Mummie, so happy." I could feel the tears on my cheeks. "I can't bear to think of you caged by that . . ."

"Hush, James," she said. "Hush, my baby." And her arm tightened around me.

The Palais had closed its doors by this time, alas, but after she'd soothed me I was able to cook us an elegant dinner of *poulet Méditerranée* with asparagus, then raspberry mousse to follow, and we listened to Benny and the divine Ella as dusk fell outside my big picture window. It was August, I believe, and I remember the evening as a long fading of golden light, as if someone were dimming the spotlight on us slowly, slowly. Our last evening together, perhaps, and I wondered how I would ever manage if my beloved Mummie could no longer come and see me. I hummed along to the dance tunes—"How High the Moon," "Stardust"—and laughed when Mummie laughed, but underneath I was distraught, in utter turmoil, sick with trepidation.

The next morning it rained, and we stayed in and did the *Observer* crossword together, or rather she did it while I sat beside her and planned, calmer now that I realized it was up to me to act for us both. I was still distraught, but my turmoil had hardened to resolve. *Per ardua ad astra.* I wasn't going to cave in. I would never again cave in to my demon father. I made her promise me just one thing before she left—that she would come back for a last visit to the flat before the ogre got his way and shut her in his den for ever.

"Don't exaggerate, James," she said, in her gentle way. "Of course I shall see you again. Only not here, not in your flat, and perhaps only for one day at a time in the future. We shall contrive, my dear. You are my son, and I shall see you."

"One last weekend, promise me, darling Mummie, please," I urged her.

"All right," she said finally, "if you insist. One final weekend, perhaps in late October before it gets really cold. I don't want to think of him alone in

Vanessa Furse Jackson

that chilly little office during the winter."

I did. Perhaps he'd do us all a favour and freeze to death.

One more chance. "You darling, darling Mummie," I said.

I didn't tell her that I'd just finished working out my last month at the studios when she came for her final weekend. They gave me a tea party on the day I left and presented me with a little replica of an Oscar that had "For Best Stand-in" engraved on its base. I couldn't have been more touched if it had been the real thing. I had a short speech prepared in case there was a gift, but when it came to it, I just broke down and cried. It was most affecting, the whole occasion.

A week later, on a cold Saturday morning in late October, Mummie arrived with a bottle of champagne to cheer us up, she said, and a large bunch of deep red and gold chrysanthemums. "Some people call them funereal flowers," she said as she handed them to me, "but I love their snuffy Edwardian scent, don't you? They live on regardless, long after summer's gone—as we shall, my darling James." She smiled at me, her courage high as always, but I knew how she must be suffering.

When she went into the spare room with her cigarettes and book for her rest after lunch, I told her I might go out for a walk, and to help herself to tea if I wasn't back when she woke up. Then I put on my anorak, my woolly hat and my fleece-lined leather gloves, and went out into the cold afternoon to face the demon.

I had everything planned out to the last detail. I was a Daniel, a David, the Jim my father wanted me to be, with my courage screwed to the sticking post and no thought of failure or cowardice. I caught the train I intended, it arrived on time, and the bitter weather allowed me to pull the hood of my anorak over my hat. Only Mummie would have recognized me as I drifted through the streets of the town that had once been my home, my container of paraffin wrapped in an old piece of carpet and concealed with some cotton wadding in an ancient rucksack.

When I reached the High Street, I walked past the front of the optician's shop to check that the slatted metal blinds were locked down over the windows and door. Heavy and old-fashioned, they had to be raised and lowered by hand, a tedious process, as I could attest. Then I went down the side alley and oh so silently let myself into the back of the shop. I'd had a set of keys copied the first Christmas I was home after his edict that I was no longer welcome there. I knew he wouldn't have changed the locks. He was too mean.

I stood in the little entry-way between the lavatory and the storeroom that was full of neatly stacked cardboard boxes and old newspapers, and I listened. I could hear the radio in his office, a voice, some wild cheering— he must have been listening to a football match. All the better. I soaked my cotton wadding, carefully poured trails of paraffin on the dusty wooden blocks of the floor, retreated to the door, and lit the match. There was plenty of time to re-lock the door, walk past the alley, through the cathedral close, and catch the train I'd planned back to Amersham.

When I reached the flat, Mummie and I had a lovely quiet spell to ourselves. We were able to drink the bottle of champagne and eat the duck *à l'orange* I'd left prepared for our dinner before two nice young police constables rang the doorbell to break the tragic news of my father's death.

"To our last weekend," I'd toasted with the first glass.

"No," she said. "No mourning the past. To us, James, darling. To our future. For there will be one, you know."

Darling, loving Mummie.

When I opened the door to the policemen, I must have presented the perfect picture of the innocent, smiling, unsuspecting and unsuspected son.

It could have happened like that. If I had really been Jim, the son my father would have made of me. If I could have acted the part.

Oh, I caught the train I intended all right. I walked through the bitter cold of the familiar town with my anorak hood pulled up. But there was no paraffin in a rucksack, no set of copied keys, no carefully worked out plan, no fire. Naturally not. I stood before the slatted metal blinds in the High Street and rapped tentatively, half-hoping he'd have forgotten I was coming. He took his time raising the door-blind far enough to negotiate the locks, but he had neither forgotten my appointment nor forgiven my existence.

When he'd locked up again, we walked through the ghostly tiers of eyeless spectacles to his office at the back of the shop. He sat behind his desk. I sat in an upright wooden chair before it, wondering if the metal ruler still lay in the same drawer between us, my loosening bowels telling me it almost certainly did.

"Well, Jim," he said finally.

"Father," I said.

On a filing cabinet behind him sat an electric kettle, three packets of Cup-a-Soup, a jar of Nescafé, and a box of Cornflakes. It was true, then. He did live here when Mummie was away visiting me. The thought lifted my flagging spirits a trifle. It was very cold in the small windowless room.

"The answer is no," my father said, straightening the blotter on his desk.

"Beg pardon?" I said.

"You have come to ask me for money," he said. "The answer is no."

"I was made redundant." I hadn't meant to confess this. "Nothing to do with the quality of my work, you understand. All the studios are cutting back. But it's not that. I thought . . ."

"You thought you would ask me to advance you part of the inheritance you assume you will be getting when I die."

I had thought to beg him to let Mummie continue her visits. She would lend me money, I knew. And she would keep her promise to see me when she could. But the thought of her never again staying the night in the spare bedroom that I kept just for her was more than I could bear. That was what had led my faltering footsteps to the ogre's den today. "No," I said. My voice broke on the word.

"Disabuse yourself of the notion," my father said. "There is no such inheritance."

Such a small, shopkeeper's mind he had. I let the silence lengthen in the airless little room. Then I said, "Please listen to me, Father." My voice remained level. I was proud of that.

"I agreed to see you," my father said, in his dry, emotionless way, "because I have something I wish to say to you." He took his fountain pen from the tray by the blotter and unscrewed the cap. Then he screwed it back on again. "Your mother's weekend visits to you must come to an end. She is no longer strong enough to venture on such excursions on her own, and I cannot allow her to exhaust herself as she does. Is that understood?"

"You knew?" He had taken me by surprise.

"That she came to you on her weekends away? Of course I did. Do you think I was born yesterday?" Really, his tone was quite unpleasant.

"You always knew?" I could hardly believe it. He'd lied to her all these years?

"I allowed the visits because I felt them to be her wish, her choice. But I am now disallowing them because I believe them to be detrimental to her health. Are you listening?" He unscrewed his pen again and examined the nib.

"But she's my mother." I felt my guts cramp, and I put my hands between my legs and bent forward for a moment.

"She's my wife," my father said in his most imperious tones. "And I will have nothing—*nothing*, do you hear me?—coming between my wife and her well-being." He screwed the cap back on his pen and laid it down on the blotter with fingers that trembled a little.

I looked at his face then. It was flushed an odd dark red, and the whites of his eyes were yellow. I found it impossible to imagine Mummie caring for such a creature. "You can't," I said.

"Oh, believe me, Jim, I can," he began.

I tried to summon strength. But my wretched insides wouldn't allow me to stand up to him as I otherwise would have. I had to bolt for the horrid little lavatory behind the office, and I know he heard the giveaway sounds of the diarrhea I was unable to control. I was humiliated, just humiliated.

On the train home, I wept, and the ticket collector asked me if I needed medical attention. I almost told him that all I needed was my mother, but I still retained some shreds of human dignity, whatever my father thought.

He died, my appalling father, about four months later. Four long months, during which I saw my poor Mummie only twice, briefly, for lunch. Heart attack in his sleep, lying next to *his wife* in the marital bed. She got rid of the bed when I came home to look after her, I'm glad to say. Said it was too big just for one person, but I knew it was the years of memories she needed to divest herself of. What a bastard the man was. What a cod-cold bastard.

But here we are, you see, happier than we've ever been, living together at long last, the demon utterly defeated. What a lucky mortal I am.

Mummie's getting older now, of course, her hair its natural grey, her figure no longer a girl's, but she's in wonderful heart. When I first moved back from Amersham, she seemed much frailer than I'd thought her when I only saw her for the restorative weekends. She must have been putting on a show for me for quite some time before I returned home, I think, as I found her enervated and listless, prone to sudden weeping and unexplained headaches. Once, I caught her with a framed photograph of my father in her

Vanessa Furse Jackson

hand, and my rage against him flared up into some unfortunate remarks for which I was forced later to apologize. It continued to smoulder, indeed, for a long while after his death. But *de mortuis nil nisi bonum* and all that.

Slowly she's grown stronger, until really now it's quite like old times. I tell her we'll go on together for years, just the two of us, reminiscing over our favourite big band tunes, enjoying our little *cordon bleu* feasts, embroidering for the cathedral on long winter evenings, and talking, talking like the best friends we are. We're almost the same age, I tell her. Like when we danced round the Palais together, everyone wondering who the perfect couple might be, whirling as one around the sprung oak floor.

She's all I need, all I want. I'm not the stand-in any more, you see. I'm the real thing. And that's my story really. Happy ever after, you might say.

Small Displacements

Susanna sat on the little gardening stool, listening to the silence vibrating in the wake of the pain. She let out a slow breath. It's back, she thought to herself, and the herb bed she was tending went quite black for a moment. There. She had acknowledged it. And now she would dismiss the knowledge. "Be gone," she said, as she would to a nettle or thistle she'd pulled up from the ground.

"What did you say, Ma?" Edward asked.

She hadn't heard him come up behind her. The herbs were sharply focused, as if each plant were edged with gold.

"What on earth's the point of weeding here?" Edward said. He laid a hand on her shoulder. "The builders are coming tomorrow to start work. Had you forgotten?"

His gentleness suggested to her that he was worried she might be going senile, which at another time would have infuriated her. "I'm not weeding, Edward," she said, without turning around. "I'm transplanting as many of the herbs as I can to the bed beyond the peas. They won't like it as much— they love the south wall of the house here. But it's too bad. I can't see where else to put them." She leaned forward again, careful to leave the pain enough room this time, and continued digging with her trowel around the clump of thyme she was working on.

"They won't survive the move," Edward said, still in that extra-patient tone that Susanna had heard him use so often in the past few weeks to his five-year-old son, Charlie. "I wish you wouldn't."

He wished she wouldn't because seeing her here fed his guilt about the building project and about his living in her house. About the entire situation, in fact. Since he was a child, Edward had shouldered guilt as if doing so would level the boulders of life he found so difficult to surmount. Susanna had a sudden vision of her herb bed as it would look tomorrow, flattened by a bulldozer, ugly, scarred earth. She dug her trowel down beside the roots of the thyme and pulled back on the handle.

"Josie wondered if you'd like some tea," Edward said, trying a different approach.

Josephine. Her daughter-in-law. In her kitchen. "Not just now, thank-you," Susanna said, pushing and rocking the mass of thyme. She inhaled its pungent oils and, incongruous in the present conversation, pictures of Sunday lunches spilled into her mind. A small joint of beef, thyme-strewn, and her father rolling up his shirtsleeves to carve. Then, after she was married, herself carving because David always said she was better at it than he, the lazy so-and-so. Susanna smiled. She saw the lovely little dining-room, whose windows looked out over the garden and the soaring hill beyond, filled with parents and aunts, cousins, friends, and, long ago, her younger sister Pam. "I have known it for seventy-two years," she said, amazed.

Edward misunderstood, of course. "Don't, Ma, don't," he said. "Don't start on that again, please. I'm sorry. I truly am sorry. But it's not as if you're really moving. You'll be popping in and out all the time, you know you will."

To pop in and out of the house in which she'd been born seemed all at once an abomination to Susanna. "Why did I ever agree?" she cried, and then stopped. What was the point? The builders were coming tomorrow. She put her hands around the ball of thyme and tugged. It came up without protest from the ground, and she buried her nose in the tiny fragrant leaves, aware that Edward had squatted down beside her.

If only having surgery was as easy, she thought. But somehow there are always roots left in the ground, waiting for the right conditions to grow again. She thought of the thyme struggling for rebirth through the concrete that would be laid over it and felt her eyes prick with tears.

"I thought you were feeling better about it," he was saying, anxiety making his voice crack like a boy's.

"I am," she said. "I am feeling better. It's just having to face it. The fact that tomorrow . ." She stopped. Better not to say anything more. "Be careful, Edward," she said. "You'll hurt your rheumaticky knee squatting like that."

She looked over at him. "You're developing quite a paunch," she added, thinking how very old we're all getting.

Edward stood up stiffly, offended. "Come and have tea when you're ready," he said, and left her to her task.

Damn, she said to herself. That was unnecessary. She laid down the thyme, shifted her stool along the path, and began working on a small rosemary bush.

The house was neither architecturally beautiful nor particularly valuable, situated as it was just too far from a good shopping town or railway or motorway access. It was a small, plain, late-Victorian house that had been built for the local estate's gamekeeper, and it tended to gather damp in the winter. But she loved it dearly—loved it passionately. Her parents had bought it in the early 1930s after her father had been forced to sell his family's Georgian, dry-rot-infested manor house because he couldn't afford its upkeep. He had mourned the loss of his old home for the rest of his life, telling her the same stories about it again and again until she feared he must have sensed her disinterest. Susanna had never wanted to live anywhere but here, where she had been born. She found it hard to imagine anyone dismissing the house as her father had. And Pam. A part of Susanna shied away from thoughts of Pam, safely distant in Santa Barbara with her pink stucco mansion, her wealthy husband, her blonde, tanned twin daughters with their perfect Californian teeth. It was providential, Susanna told herself firmly, that Pam had renounced any claim to this house—had removed herself so completely.

The rosemary was going to be more difficult than the thyme. She scooped out a trowel-full of earth from around the roots, then another and another. The pain was pressing low down against her spine. She ignored it.

But Pam was not so easily put out of mind. Susanna sighed. Her parents had never spared telling her how badly she'd behaved when Pam was born, but what Susanna remembered, had never been able to erase, was the terrible hurt she'd carried around within her, which her beloved parents had been unable (unwilling, she'd felt at the time) to heal. She'd been eight when she was taken to the hospital to bring Mummy home, and no one—she swore this all her life—no one had warned her of the baby who was coming home to live also. I must have been a holy terror, she'd often thought since, but the echo of the hurt could still sound its hollow note of exclusion even now.

She wanted to associate the house with happiness, and, as she used her fingers to remove the dirt from around the roots, she forced her mind forward to David, even though there was hurt there, too. She'd been almost forty when she married him, her lovely David, the lover she'd been so afraid she'd never have. In her mind, and vividly in her dreams, she could still put her arms around his broad chest, hold him tight, tight.

They had nominally lived in a flat in Manchester, where he was from, for a few months after they were married, but for much of that time she was living at home, helping her mother to nurse her father through his last illness, then watching her mother fade as fast as she could to follow him in a matter of weeks. "I have a crisis here," Pam had said from California. "Otherwise I'd be right over. But I trust you to cope, Susie. You'll do a grand job, and I'm sure Mummy would much rather have you than me anyway." Susanna had believed nothing Pam had said.

It had been a bewildering, unhappy time, but much of it had been blotted out by the early years afterwards when, astonishingly, the house was hers. David had been only too glad to move here, writing and reviewing books, taking over the vegetable garden, helping her to scrimp and save (there had never been quite enough money), and sharing in the care of Edward. Conceiving and bearing a healthy child when she was over forty had seemed to Susanna an extraordinary blessing, and they both unashamedly adored Edward, though David worried about his being an only child, perhaps becoming spoiled. But she had refused to risk another, less perfect baby. "Another baby would upset Edward," she said to David. "Trust me. I know."

Edward was a dear, Susanna thought now, but from a serious little boy, forever worried he'd done something that would displease the parents he worshipped, he'd become a serious and, she admitted to herself, rather stolid grown man, forever apologizing to his wife. Josephine.

She tugged gently at the bush, but the rosemary remained rooted in the ground.

Susanna had liked Josephine so much the first time Edward brought her down for a weekend visit. She'd enjoyed the way the couple interacted, touched each other, laughed. Josephine had a radiant air to her. She wore scarlet and sapphire and bright yellow and smelled deliciously of jasmine. She seemed to wake up something in the little house that had slept since David's death. Susanna had never seen Edward in such a glow, and she was so glad and relieved that this love had come to him that she remembered thanking Josephine profusely, probably embarrassingly, before they left.

She'd continued to be glad and to like Josephine until—well, until when? The conversation she'd overheard shortly after the wedding, on another weekend visit it must have been, had shaken her. "Susanna's such an unsuitable name for a mother-in-law," she'd heard Josephine saying, laughing about it to Edward. "I'm never going to be able to call her that—I know I'm not." And she hadn't. She never addressed her as Susanna in conversation— somehow avoided having to address her at all—and wrote in cards and letters to My dearest Mother-in-law, which Susanna had found humorous at first and then faintly annoying.

But she hadn't really minded, had she? Edward was happy—ecstatic when Charlie was born—and she saw all of them no more than twice or three times a year. Edward came more often and had been marvellous when she was ill, so it wasn't as if she'd lost him. There was just, in the shadow of her thoughts, a dissatisfaction that she hadn't managed to get closer to Josephine or to love her more unreservedly. It chafed her that Josephine (like Pam, she thought unwillingly) represented a kind of failure of self. Josephine made her feel less than whole, as if an essential piece of her were missing or inactive. *Was that why I invited them to live here?* she thought. She stood up carefully and moved the stool to the other side of the rosemary bush. It felt precarious sitting there in the earth of the herb bed, but she was determined to lose as little as possible to the builders. The destroyers.

When David had died, she'd been too enmeshed in grief for several years to think much about her financial state, but when she'd become ill, she'd realized that she no longer wanted to die and had started to pay attention to the future. She'd sought advice, planned carefully, and believed herself secure, even if there was little to spare. Then the markets fell and there was less to spare, then less than that. The house, she was told, might have to go—and really she'd be much better off in a small flat nearer to health centres and shops and that vaguely frightening word, help.

In a panic, she rang Edward and suggested that he think about coming to live in the house, which she would make over to him absolutely if he would undertake to build a small extension in which she could live separately from them. When he and Josephine agreed to the scheme, she'd felt a vast relief that she was saved, that the house was saved for her. It was only gradually, and

Vanessa Furse Jackson

partly because of the reactions of friends, that she began to think of her offer as having been made less out of necessity than out of generosity—generosity not only to Edward but also to Josephine, the daughter-in-law she seemed unable to reach. Even in the initial panic, she thought now, somewhere at the back of her mind had been the notion that Josephine would be grateful and would think more of her for giving them her beloved house.

The rosemary was beginning to tilt, its roots almost completely exposed. Susanna leant forward with caution, grasped the main stem, and pulled. She twisted, pulled again, and the bush gave way with a crack like a green bone breaking. She turned over the bush and, sure enough, one of the main roots showed a torn white stump. "Damn," she said, laying the bush down beside the thyme and the other limp piles of herbs that Edward had mistaken for weeds. She leant forward and closed her eyes for a moment. "Damn." She waited while the pain pulsed.

What had never occurred to her—and she found her obtuseness incomprehensible in hindsight—was what it would feel like to share her house with people who were no longer guests but permanent residents. For Edward and Josephine and Charlie had moved in almost straight away, Edward remaining in their flat in Manchester (where he lectured in nineteenth-century literature at the university) during the week and coming down to the house every weekend. He and Josephine, he said, wanted to take the burden of overseeing architects and builders off her shoulders. They would cope with all that. She wasn't to worry any more. Susanna tried to be grateful for this, but the process was insufferably slow, something else she hadn't envisaged. It might be another year before she could move into her granny flat, as Edward would insist on calling it.

So there was Josephine in her kitchen, Josephine taking over the ironing, Josephine buying strange foods instead of using the vegetables and herbs from the garden, Josephine playing horrible contemporary jazz on the so-called entertainment system they had brought with them. And Charlie, whom Susanna had loved for his likeness to David and his infectious laugh, seemed to have become another child now he was living with her. He watched television—far too much, she thought—in the suddenly cramped sitting-room and screamed when it was time to go to school or to bed. Unsettled by the move and by the weekday absences of his father, he followed her around when she wanted to be alone, asking the inane, extended questions that had seemed so charming when Edward had been that age. Simultaneously, she longed for the extension to be finished and dreaded the move away from everything familiar. How much of her treasured furniture and pictures and books would have to be left behind in the house?

She began to understand how hard it must have been for her father to lose his childhood home, the places and objects he had loved—how diminished he must have felt by the new circumstances forced upon him. She wished she could retract the disinterest she'd shown and talk to him about it. She longed to connect with people who'd had to leave cherished homes, wanting to feel linked to other communities of loss.

"Did you know," she'd said to Edward about a month after the occupation began, "that soon after your grandparents moved here the Haweswater Reservoir was constructed?"

They were sitting together on the wooden bench at the end of the garden, sharing the *Sunday Times*, while Josephine was stuffing a butterflied leg of lamb and Charlie was watching cartoons. Edward was deep into the book reviews. "Mmm?" he said.

"To provide water for Manchester," she went on.

"To what?" Edward said, still reading.

"And that in order to do so, they had to flood an entire village?"

"No, I didn't know that," Edward said.

"Mardale, the village was called. Drowned. Obliterated. All those people just told to leave. Can you imagine?"

"No, I can't," Edward said warily and stopped reading.

"What would it feel like to lose your home like that? Never to go back?"

"Well, you're hardly in the same situation, Ma," Edward said.

"Or Imber," his mother went on as if he hadn't spoken.

"Imber?" he said.

"The village on Salisbury Plain that was evacuated when the army requisitioned it in 1943."

"How do you know all this?" Edward asked.

"I went online, of course," she said, impatiently. "One hundred and forty-three people given six weeks notice to leave their homes."

"Online?" Edward said in disbelieving tones.

"They were promised they could return at the end of the war, but the

Vanessa Furse Jackson

promise was broken. The army still uses the ruined houses to train soldiers to fight in built-up areas. I'm not completely stupid, you know, Edward," she said, her voice so sharp that he began to apologize profusely.

She cut him short. "They're allowed back once a year to tend to the graves in the churchyard," she said. "Those who are still alive."

Rather a low blow that, she thought to herself, getting up slowly from the little stool. She bent to pick up the herbs, waiting for the pain to grip, but it remained quiet for the moment. Grateful, she put each plant into the wheelbarrow with as much care as if she were handling newborns, holding up their precious heads, smoothing their limbs.

"What are you doing?" asked Charlie.

She hadn't heard him come, and she started as if he had caught her in an illegal act. "I'm moving these herbs, darling. Careful, you're standing on some mint."

"Why?" he said without moving.

"So that they don't get hurt when the men come to start the building tomorrow." She could hear in her voice the same patient tone that had annoyed her in Edward. She pushed Charlie gently off the mint and bent to pick it up. Pain jolted through her. She straightened slowly, bringing the bruised leaves to her face to breathe in their fragrance. She remembered her mother cutting the same leaves into summer salads with a pair of sharp scissors shaped like a flying bird, the kitchen bathed in minty scent. Josephine liked garlic in her salads.

"Why?" Charlie said again, as if she hadn't spoken.

"Why what?"

He considered her with David's slanting blue eyes. "I do like you, Granny," he said.

"Well, thank you," she said, warmed.

"But I wish I could go back home," he went on. "There's no one to play with here." He let out a noisy sigh. "No one just for me."

"Oh, Charlie," Susanna said, forgetting her pain as she knelt down beside him. "I'm so, so sorry." She put her arms and the tangle of mint around him. "I wish you could go back, too," she said to him.

"Hello there," said Josephine, from somewhere above them.

Susanna got up too quickly and clenched her teeth.

"Come and have some tea, you two," said Josephine, neatly pairing her with her child, Susanna noted. "I've made a cake. Lemon icing. I thought we'd celebrate."

Charlie ran back into the house with a shout, but Susanna said, "Thank you. How kind. I shall be in just as soon as I've seen to these herbs." *Celebrate the beginning of the building work?* she thought. *How could she be so insensitive?*

Josephine stood looking at her, silent for once. She was wearing jeans and an old gray T-shirt with flour down the front of it. Susanna thought she looked pale and tired and said, surprising herself, "I'm sorry. This is hard on you, I know."

"Do you?" said Josephine.

"We've all been displaced by this in one way or another, haven't we?" Susanna said, pleased, a little amazed, that she could feel this compassion for Josephine.

"Pretty small displacements," Josephine said. "I'd hardly count myself a fleeing refugee, would you?" She smiled, but Susanna thought her voice distant. "Come in when you're ready then." She turned and went back into the house.

Edward had had a similar response when Susanna had tried reopening the topic with him last weekend. As she wheeled her barrow full of herbs and the trowel and the little stool down to the vegetable garden, she wondered if Josephine had overheard their conversation. More likely he her told about it later, she reasoned, disturbed at the idea of being discussed, especially unfavourably, by her son.

Stupid to bring it up again really, to worry at it as one might at a loose tooth. And unfair on Edward. She hadn't meant to upset him.

"Perhaps I'll start writing great poetry when I've moved into my little flat," she had said jokingly. Charlie had been lured to bed by the promise of a story later from Daddy, and Josephine was upstairs bathing him, so she and Edward were alone.

He hadn't immediately responded.

"Like Byron and Shelley displaced to the shores of Lake Geneva," she'd gone on. "Or Browning in Pisa, or was it Florence?"

"For heaven's sake," Edward had exploded, banging his whisky glass down on the table beside his chair so hard that drops flew out from it in a tawny arc. "Once and for all, will you stop talking about yourself as if you were about to become a displaced person?"

"Careful," she said. "You'll leave marks on the polish."

Edward scrubbed angrily at the table-top with his handkerchief. "A displaced person is a person removed from home by military events or political pressure," he said, in a tone that suggested she should be taking notes. "As you know, or as you certainly ought to know, millions of people, many of them Jews, were displaced after World War Two. Literally displaced. Wanderers, without a place to go."

"Yes, I know, Edward," she began.

"So camps were established for them," he went on over her. "And do you know where many of these camps were located? On the sites of concentration camps. Death camps. What do you think about that, eh?" He snorted down a gulp of whisky.

"I'm not meaning to compare myself," Susanna began again.

"Yes, you *are!*" Edward shouted, then cleared his throat. "Sorry." Lowering his voice, he went on, "Most of the Jewish DPs were kept behind barbed-wire and watched over by guards. The conditions were appalling, and many of them died from disease or malnutrition. You can't just fling the term around as if it had none of those connotations."

"I'm not meaning to fling anything," she said, tiredly. "I'm just trying to tell you how I feel."

"Right now," Edward said, with professorial authority, "there are estimated to be around twenty-five million people displaced because of conflict inside their own countries. Twenty-five million, most of them women and children. IDPs—internally displaced persons. And that's not even counting the millions who are international refugees. Millions more, my God."

"How do you know all that?" she asked him.

He looked a bit sheepish. "I was doing some electronic research for a paper I'm writing," he said, "so while I was online, well . . . " and they were both able to laugh for a moment. But he still wouldn't allow her her point. "We are in no way displacing you," he said. "You aren't going to any other place."

"Even small moves can hurt," she said. "Wasn't it John Clare who went mad after moving from the cottage of his birth to another only eight miles away?"

"Three miles. From Helpston to Northborough. And no, that wasn't what caused his mental problems. Not by itself, anyway. Let's drop it, shall we?" He got up to refill his whisky glass, and Susanna said no more. But her mind would not be quieted.

She'd already cleared a little patch of earth behind the peas, and although she was tiring she decided to plant the herbs before she went in for tea, so as to keep them out of the ground for the shortest possible time. And to avoid Josephine—clearly upset about something—and the cake with lemon icing. She sighed. "I should simply have stuck it out," she muttered, as she sat down on the stool and thrust her trowel into the earth. *Careful*, she imagined the pain saying. *Be very careful now*.

If it really had come back (and you don't yet know that it has, she admonished herself), there would be decisions to make about whether to accept treatment this time, whether and when to tell Edward, or whether to simply drive her car very fast into the supports of a sturdy bridge. She'd promised herself that's what she'd do if it ever did return, but now she didn't feel so sure. She hastily blotted from her mind a picture of Edward standing in an icy morgue identifying her smashed, animalistic remains. She bent forward and set a sprawl of mint into the ground, then pressed earth around its roots to hold it. She sat back. It certainly did look weakened by the move, the leaves pale and drooping as if drained of blood. She sighed again, hoping Edward's prognosis was wrong. Moving the stool each time, she dug more holes and tenderly laid the tarragon and the thyme, the parsley and dill, sage, lemon balm, marjoram and chives, into their new places, coaxing and encouraging each plant as she did so.

She breathed in the herbs' scents one by one, as if they could protect her against the plague of memories that recalled those awful treatments, treatments that steadily increased in awfulness until just getting into the car for the hour and a half's drive to the hospital would make her nauseous. *I can't go through that again*, she thought fiercely. *I won't*. And there was only one proper bathroom in the house, dear God. She picked a leaf of lemon balm and crushed its oils in her fingers, breathing in and in until the thoughts and images were diffused by the tang of herbal citrus.

She had to dig a bigger hole for the wounded rosemary, and, as she jabbed her trowel into the ground, she told herself she was jabbing at the disease, at the idea of having the disease, that she would not allow it to grow within her, that all the spaces would be filled with compassion and good

Vanessa Furse Jackson

will and love, and there would be No Room for anything else. She would not be diminished. The hole made, she picked up the rosemary and almost triumphantly set it into its new home. "You'll heal and grow down here behind the peas, do you hear me?" she said, scraping and pressing earth back around it. Above the smell of the turned soil, the air was thick with its spiky scent.

Susanna got up from the stool, uncurling her spine with care. She rubbed her lower back where the pain pushed and thought of all the gardening she'd been doing lately because gardening kept her busy and out of the house. She'd probably strained her back. It was probably no more than that.

She pushed the wheelbarrow to the old tap by the shed and filled the big watering can she'd left there. As the water splashed, she stood for a moment, looking down the garden at the sweep of the hill beyond, soft with green wheat just now, curving like a wave up to its white froth of hawthorn blossom at the top of the field. Had Pam minded leaving the house, the country where she'd grown up? She'd never asked her.

She trundled the barrow back to the herbs, lifted the heavy can up, and began to tip the water around the new transplants. "There," she said. "There."

It took two more trips until she was satisfied that each plant was sufficiently watered, and when she'd finished, she was stiff with weariness. She went to the wooden bench at the end of the garden and sat down to examine the ache of exclusion that still lay within her. It had to do with why she'd upset Edward earlier. About becoming old, about *feeling* old, about feeling she'd been unwillingly herded into the land of the old when that is not at all how she felt inside. Was that it? She turned the thought over, as if it were an object, a strange plant or shell, that she was trying to identify. The old are not us. The old are our parents and grandparents. The old are the grey and nodding ones in the supermarket who wheel so slowly up and down the aisles that we want to scream and run them over. The old get moved from houses too big for them into nice little granny flats. Old people's homes. They get ill and afraid. They are exiled from the land of the young, from the land that defines them, into an alien country where the ultimate displacement awaits.

Susanna could hear the back door of the house open. Someone was coming to look for her. There wasn't much time. *I invited them to come and live in my house*, she thought, urgently. *And now I am facing the prospect of my own emigration, at which I am outraged. Sorrowful*, she amended, but honesty insisted, *outraged. And I have behaved accordingly.* In a moment of clarity, she saw the difficult, distant, unwelcoming figure she must have presented. A ridiculous figure, as she recognized now. *God knows*, she thought, *what stresses and fractures have been built in to all of our relationships. What would David make of the person I have become?*

When Edward reached her, she was in tears on the wooden bench, and for the second time that day, she heard him say, "Don't, Ma, don't. I'm sorry, I'm so sorry," as he sat down beside her.

"No," she was able to say, collecting herself. "No, Edward, it's all right. Really." She fished for a tissue and blew her nose. "I think I've been making a fool of myself these past weeks." She waited for him to deny this.

Edward looked at her uncertainly. "You're upset about tomorrow," he said.

"I'm afraid," Susanna said, wiping her eyes. She wanted to awaken his sympathy and thought about telling him of the return of the pain.

Edward put his arm around her and they sat still for a moment. "I promised Josie I'd get you inside for some tea," he said.

"And home-made cake," she said, standing up with some difficulty. The trouble was that telling him would also awaken his guilt, and she wasn't sure she could bear that. Edward linked an arm in hers, and she allowed him to move her towards the house. "Do you think my herbs will recover?" she asked, pausing at the little bed.

"They look a bit wobbly, don't they?" Edward said. "But perhaps they will live after all." As they stood there, looking down at the plants, he said in his awkward Edward way, "She's pregnant, you know."

"Oh my God," Susanna blurted out before she could stop herself.

"Yes, I thought that's what you'd say," said Edward, despondently unlinking his arm from hers.

"No, Edward, you misunderstood. I meant, oh my God, that was why the cake with lemon icing." But what she was thinking was *oh, my poor Charlie*.

"You've lost me," he said.

"And I've been out here all this time, as if trying to avoid her. No," she said, "deliberately avoiding her."

"I'm so sorry it had to happen now," said Edward. "It's the worst possible timing, I know."

"Is that what you said to her?" Susanna asked.

"Josie knew you'd be upset," he said, watching her.

"No wonder she's looking tired."

"You don't mind?" he said, still unsure of her.

Susanna looked at him. "Do you think," she said, "that if I started calling her Josie, she might be able to call me Susanna?"

"You do mind," said Edward. His eyelids drooped unhappily. "Oh Ma, what are we going to do?"

"Survive," she said. "What else can we do?" She put both arms around him, exerting no pressure, and allowed herself, for a brief moment, the comfort of her son's broad chest.

Vanessa Furse Jackson comes originally from England. However, married to an Ohio native, she's been resident in the United States for over twenty years and currently lives and writes in South Texas, where she teaches English at Texas A&M University-Corpus Christi.

A book about her great grandfather, *The Poetry of Henry Newbolt: Patriotism Is Not Enough,* was published in 1994 by ELT Press, and her first collection of stories, *What I Cannot Say to You,* was published in 2003 by the University of Missouri Press.